The Warrior and the Bride

Ray Filby

The Warrior and the Bride

Publisher : Midhurst

Published by Midhurst

Copyright © Ray Filby 2022

This is a work of fiction.
Apart from obvious historic characters,
any resemblance to actual persons,
living or dead, is purely coincidental.

Midhurst.
2, Freers Mews,
Warwick,
Warwickshire,
CV34 6DP

ISBN

http://midhurstpublishing.uk

Acknowledgements

The author would like to thank Denise Smith for designing and painting the cover picture.

The author is also indebted to his wife, Sue, both for proof reading and for her patience and encouragement during the writing of this story.

Contents

Introduction		9
Chapter 1	Flight from Gilboa	11
Chapter 2	Ziklag	17
Chapter 3	An Appraisal of David	26
Chapter 4	Consolidation of David's Kingdom	33
Chapter 5	Jerusalem	43
Chapter 6	Benaiah's Prowess	58
Chapter 7	Continuing War against the Ammonites	66
Chapter 8	Amnon and Tamar	74
Chapter 9	Gilgal and Machpelah	86
Chapter 10	Thoughts held regarding the future of Israel	105
Chapter 11	Absalom's Rebellion	114
Chapter 12	Shimei and Sheba	135
Chapter 13	Abishag and Eglah	138
Chapter 14	Further War with the Philistines	145
Chapter 15	David's Last Days	148
Chapter 16	Solomon Consolidates his New Status	158

Chapter 17	The Wedding	167
Chapter 18	Reign of King Solomon	178
Appendix 1	List of Characters	188
Appendix 2	Genealogies and Family Trees	191
Appendix 3	Map of Israel	199
Appendix 4	Biblical References	201
Appendix 5	Bibliography	207

Introduction

While this work of Biblical fiction has been written with an audience in mind of those who are interested in Biblical history, the author hopes that others will also find this tale of an extended romance set in a period of unrest and tumult to be an interesting read.

The story is largely set in the 2nd Book of Samuel and the 1st Book of Kings, and the author has tried to include the Biblical background in a way which doesn't interfere too seriously with the flow of the story. In the interest of keeping the book consistent with the Bible, the author has needed to include a large number of characters. Many of these are fairly minor but a separate list of characters has been included as an appendix which may prove helpful to the reader in keeping track of characters which recur in the story. The reader may well find it useful to read this story alongside the two Biblical books which provided the historic context of this story.

The main characters are Benaiah and Abishag, two individuals who had important roles to play in serving King David and his successor. Although a work of fiction, hopefully, the story is consistent with the Biblical narrative and references are provided wherever the story is related to a Biblical event. The author realises that minor inconsistencies do occur in the text but then, minor inconsistencies can be found in the Bible itself. There is no indication in the Bible that the two main characters were in any way related but nothing in the Bible specifically states that they were not.

Attitudes and beliefs have been ascribed to the two main characters which are well ahead of the Old Testament culture in which they were living. Their attitudes are indeed, ahead of current Jewish thought, especially in their understanding of God's declaration to Abraham, that through his offspring, all nations of earth will be blessed because he had obeyed God. (Genesis ch 22 v 18). This is a repeat of a promise God had made to Abraham earlier in the book of Genesis (ch 12 v 3).

Chapter 1

Flight from Gilboa

The room echoed to an urgent banging on the door. The sun had not yet risen. A woman whose face was etched with anxiety rushed to the door and opened it. She flung herself into the arms of the man who had knocked.

"I've been so anxious for your safety," she said, trying to conceal the agitation in her voice. The agitation was mingled with relief. "You said you'd be home much sooner than this. I've waited for you all night. I'd hoped to see you by yesterday at the latest. This had been the plan."

The woman was Jerusha who was now being held in the arms of her husband, Jehoiada. Jehoiada was a soldier from the army of King Saul. Jehoiada didn't prolong the embrace.

"Quick, rouse the boy and get some possessions packed," ordered Jehoiada. "I'll saddle the donkey. We must leave here immediately. At daybreak, the place will be swarming with Philistines. We'll travel south. I'll fill you in with what happened yesterday and my plans for our future on our journey."

Jerusha immediately sensed the urgency of the situation. She went into the neighbouring room to wake Benaiah, their son.

"Quick, Benaiah, get dressed as quickly as you can. Your father's home. It's clear we're in danger. We must leave this place as soon as possible."

Although Jerusha spoke quietly, just above a whisper, there was an urgency in her tone to which Benaiah responded. He quickly put on some clothes, gathered a few things into a bag and was ready to go as Jehoiada brought the donkey round to the front door. They carried out the few possessions Jerusha had managed to gather into a large bag and they loaded these on to the donkey. With that, they started their southward journey, Jeshua riding and the menfolk walking by her side. Benaiah was a strongly built young lad, just into his teens.

Jehoiada began to talk about the battle which had waged the day before on the slopes of Mount Gilboa[1].

"We were vastly outnumbered by the Philistines. We hadn't expected so many this far north of their normal territory. Saul has been so busy trying to seek out David that he hasn't paid attention to the plain of Esdraelon which the Philistines must have crossed to reach

Gilboa. I'd entered into one to one combat with a Philistine and came within an inch of losing my own life but with God's help, I got the upper hand and finished him off. By then, the battle had moved on. I was way behind Philistine lines with no chance of being able to re-join Saul's army. I could see them being cut to pieces by the Philistines. I watched for just a few moments longer but then I could see that all was lost. Our men were fleeing before the advancing Philistines. Even now, the Philistines may be into Shunem, pillaging and plundering. I had no alternative but to return home and get you both to safety."

"What about Saul and his sons?" asked Jerusha. "You say that they're good fighters. Did they escape?"

"I can't say," replied Jehoiada, "but I think it unlikely. We were overwhelmingly outnumbered, perhaps ten to one. For all their prowess, the odds would have been very much against them. There's a limit to what can be achieved against so many!"

"Where are we going now?" asked Benaiah. He was used to the upheavals of military life, having been brought up in the family of a prominent warrior at a time when the nation of Israel was passing through a phase of continuous and prolonged warfare. The Philistines weren't Israel's only enemies in the fierce competition to control the land between the Jordan and the Great Sea (Mediterranean). This was contested by the Midianites, the Moabites, the Ammonites and the Amalekites, to say nothing of the many smaller Canaanite tribes which had occupied that land when it was known as Canaan. This was before the Israelites under Joshua had invaded from the south to lay claim to the territory God had granted by a covenant agreement with the nation's patriarch, Abraham.[2] Benaiah's family's hurried departure from their most recent home was a recurrent experience as these wars seemed to be never-ending.

"My plan is to join David," explained Jehoiada. "It's well known that he's already been anointed king by no less a person than Samuel[3]. Should anything have happened to Saul, he'll be the undisputed king of Israel."

"Where's David now? What route are you planning to follow to get to him?" asked Jerusha.

"He's believed to be way down south at Ziklag, which lies just to the west of the Salt Sea (Dead Sea). We'll follow a route through the territories of Manasseh, Ephraim and Benjamin. That should give us safe passage. All going well, we'll reach Shechem before the end of the day. We can take stock of our situation when we're there. Someone should be able to give us more definite information on David's whereabouts."

As the sun rose, they could appreciate the lie of the land around them. They were travelling through hill country well to the east of the coastal plain. As they travelled, they caught up with another refugee family. Jehoiada recognised the man, Elhanan, a fellow soldier in Saul's army. He too had become isolated from the main army in yesterday's fighting and was fleeing with his family from Shunem. Jehoiada had indicated to Jerusha that Shunem would be overrun by the Philistines a day or so after the battle of Gilboa. Elhanan was travelling with his wife, Acsah, his son Zalmon, and daughter, Abishag. Zalmon was much of an age with Benaiah. Abishag was somewhat younger. The two families continued their journey together. There was safety in numbers. The young people proved good company for each other as they made their way south.

In contrast to the turmoil the families had experienced earlier in the day as they had made a hurried departure from their homes, they now felt a sense of peace. This was tinged with a little anxiety as they travelled away from the theatre of war. The sun had risen over the hills to the east and the shadows of the scattered clouds, driven by the westerly breeze, scurried before them like migrating herds of tiny creatures, swarming across the low hillocks that characterised the country through which they were passing. They replenished their water bottles as they crossed the streams which flowed eastwards to feed the Jordan. As they climbed to higher ground, they occasionally caught sight of this river which marked the eastern boundary of their land. It reflected the sun's rays and glistened silver as it meandered its way south towards the Salt Sea which was near their destination.

They reached Shechem later in the day where they rested overnight before continuing their journey to join David. It was confirmed by the people of Shechem that Ziklag was indeed David's current headquarters. The following evening, they reached Ziklag.

Chapter 2

Ziklag

When Jehoiada and Elhanan and their families arrived at Ziklag, they were surprised to see the chaotic state of the settlement. Smouldering heaps indicated sites where there had once been buildings. New tents were being erected to replace the shelter which would have been previously provided by the burnt out buildings. There were very few women around. The men seemed agitated, upset and some showed signs of being very angry.

Jehoiada and Elhanan found a site where they could erect their own tents while Jerusha and Acsah foraged for some food.

"It's late and we're tired. Let's eat now and get some sleep," counselled Jehoiada. "In the morning, Elhanan and I will investigate what's going on. Clearly, some sort of catastrophe has overtaken the place."

The following morning, Jehoiada and Elhanan mixed with the people to discover what had happened. They returned to their tents after a couple of hours to explain the situation.

"It appears that David and his men have only just returned after being away for several weeks in the service of Achish, King of Gath," Jehoiada explained. "A few days ago, Ziklag was raided by the Amalekites who plundered the place and have taken all the women and children away as captives. Some of the men are furious with David for leaving the settlement so inadequately defended while they were away. They've even spoken of lynching David.[4] Tempers have calmed a little and David has held a war council with the leaders of his army. The Amalekites have left a fairly clear trail to be followed. David has sought divine guidance by consulting Abiathar, the priest, who has given him clear instructions that he should immediately pursue the Amalekite raiding party.[5] The plan is to go in pursuit as soon as the army are provisioned and ready. Elhanan and I intend to set out with David's men."

"Can we come too," implored Benaiah and Zalmon, anxious to be involved in the action. Their mothers protested that they shouldn't be allowed to do this but Jehoiada and Elhanan encouraged the boys.

"Benaiah and Zalmon are now in their teens," the fathers explained. "We started to follow the army when we were their age, perhaps even younger. In view of their youth, they'll be allocated a fairly safe place from which to observe any battle which may take place. Trust us to make sure they're well protected. In view of the dangerous and unsettled times in which we live, the sooner the boys become accustomed to being in a war zone, the better."

So it was, Jehoiada and Elhanan sought out the military leaders to offer the service of themselves and their sons in the campaign which was to follow. This service was gladly accepted. When the commanders discovered that they had been fighting the Philistines with Saul's army in the north, they took them to David to brief him on the state of the conflict there. Jehoiada and Elhanan had little good news to report. They explained how they had been left behind when the fighting passed them by as a huge Philistine army surrounded the relatively small force of Saul and Jonathan. David was anxious to learn how Saul and Jonathan had fared but Jehoiada and Elhanan knew nothing definite and were reluctant to express their pessimism to David.

David and his six hundred best men along with Jehoiada and Elhanan, and Benaiah and Zalmon, set out to find the Amalekites. Jehoiada and Elhanan had their own swords but Benaiah and Zalmon were equipped with a bow each and a quiver full of arrows from the weapons store at Ziklag. They felt thrilled to be marching out with David's army. An apprehensive

Jerusha and Acsah, along with Abishag, waved to them as the fighting men (and boys) passed by. The track left by the Amalekites was easy to follow until they came to the Besor Ravine later that day. They crossed this with some difficulty but after the rigours of continuous campaigning for many months and the long march, two hundred of David's men sank to the ground exhausted.[6] It was clear that if they were to make good time in their pursuit of the Amalekites, they would have to continue with a diminished army.

David continued with four-hundred men but began to lose the track as they started to traverse hard ground. David surveyed the terrain.

"There are three directions in which they could have gone," he declared to his officers. "They may have turned east towards the Jordan valley, continued northwards or moved westwards towards the land of the Philistines. We'll need to send out three small reconnaissance parties to search out these three possibilities before continuing with the main force. We don't want to waste time and energy going in the wrong direction."

Within the hour, the reconnaissance party investigating the northward route returned with a man who looked in very poor shape but who said he could lead them to the

Amalekite camp. Scouts were sent out to recall the other two reconnaissance parties.

It was necessary to give this poor man food and water to enable him to recover before he was in a fit state to be of much help. It turned out that this man was the Egyptian slave of one of the Amalekite chieftains. He had been abandoned by his master when he became ill. This Egyptian was obviously very nervous, believing that he was in danger from these Israelites but he was prepared to direct David's men to the Amalekites on condition that they meant him no harm and that they wouldn't return him to his Amalekite master.[7]

He led David through the hill country and after a final stiff climb, they reached the brow of one of a series of ridges they were traversing. They discovered that the Amalekite camp was visible from this vantage point. The camp was sprawled out right across the valley. Unaware of the proximity of the pursuing army, the Amalekites were drinking and revelling, enjoying the huge amount of plunder these marauders had taken during their recent raids.

David ordered the army to take up battle positions. The archers, which included Benaiah and Zalmon, were placed in the front rank, just ahead of the spearmen. The main force of swordsmen stood behind the spearmen. It was explained to Benaiah and Zalmon that the battle would start by their firing volleys of arrows into the Amalekites who were well within range of the bow. This would provoke the Amalekites to either flee or make a frontal attack, hoping to reach the Israelites before being cut down by the arrows. As soon as the Amalekites got near, the bowmen would drop back behind the spearmen who would present an impenetrable wall of spears. The Amalekites would find it difficult to fight through the spearmen. Once the Amalekite charge had been checked by the spearmen, the spearmen would step aside, allowing the swordsmen through to continue the battle.

It took a little while before the Amalekites suddenly became aware of the hostile Israelite army on the brow of the ridge and massed into battle formation. The battle followed the plan which had been explained to Benaiah and Zalmon. Although they couldn't tell whether their individual arrows from among the volleys which were fired, had found a target in the form of an Amalekite warrior, the boys were pleased to see that the range of their arrows was no less than that of the experienced archers around them. Benaiah and Zalmon were both strong lads and could draw their bows as fully as their senior counterparts to attain a good range. They were encouraged by the plaudits of the archers around them who could see how well these boys were doing.

As the Amalekites approached, the commander of archers ordered them to take three paces backwards as the spearmen moved forward. The Amalekite advance stopped as they reached the row of spears which confronted them and the spearmen followed a manoeuvre in which alternate spearmen moved behind their neighbour, enabling the swordsmen to rush forward to engage the Amalekites in fierce hand to hand fighting. The Israelites were winning all along the line but not without receiving casualties. The spearman in front of Benaiah was killed by an Amalekite warrior who had managed to penetrate the line of swordsmen. He in turn was confronted by an Israelite swordsman but the Israelite tripped and fell. The Amalekite raised his sword to finish off the fallen soldier but Benaiah who had been keenly watching the contest, picked up the fallen spearman's weapon and charged the Amalekite, hitting him squarely in the chest. The Amalekite was protected by his armour but fell back, winded by the blow Benaiah had inflicted. By this time, the Israelite swordsman was back on his feet and had the advantage now over the winded Amalekite whom he quickly dispatched.

The battle had started quite late in the evening and now it was dusk and distinguishing friend from foe was becoming increasingly difficult. A trumpet sounded from the Amalekite camp and the Amalekites withdrew. The swordsmen whom Benaiah had saved rushed over to congratulate this young lad and took note of his father's name. He would make a point of meeting him later.

The Israelite army was commanded to rest and get some sleep in preparation for the continuing battle which would take place on the morrow. Sentries were posted along the Israelite lines to forestall any possibility of a surprise night attack from the Amalekites. Fires were lit, warm drinks prepared and food distributed among the resting soldiers.

The battle resumed at daybreak but the Israelites were now well on top and slaughtered the Amalekites who continued to offer resistance. A hundred or so Amalekites, seeing the battle was lost, retreated to their camels and fled.

On entering the Amalekite camp, the Israelites were relieved to discover that all the women captured by the Amalekites were safe, unharmed and well including David's two wives, Ahinoam and Abigail. The Amalekites had abandoned immense amounts of plunder including flocks of cattle, sheep and goats taken from the many communities whom the marauding Amalekites had raided over recent months. The Israelites gathered all this up and set off on their return to Ziklag with the women that had been rescued from the Amalekites.[8] Benaiah and Zalmon were in a state of euphoria as they made their return journey, marching with the battle-hardened troops of David's army. They had experienced their first battle and had acquitted themselves well.

Chapter 3

An Appraisal of David

Hindered by the slow moving cattle they had recovered from the Amalekite camp, it took some little while for David's four hundred men to get back to the Besor Ravine where two hundred of their colleagues had been left on the outward march.

Benaiah had heard so much about David. He was very much a hero to the men who served him. His courage and prowess at defeating the Philistine giant, Goliath, had become folklore. Some cynics who wanted to detract from David's reputation, declared that in a contest between a giant, armed only with close combat weapons, and a lad, who was skilled in using long distance weapons like a sling or a bow and arrow, they would always favour the lad.

David had shown himself to be an inspiring and decisive commander, both in the battle which had just taken place with the Amalekites and the preparation for this. He was full of confidence as he moved among his men, encouraging them and assuring them of success.

It was known that the great priest and prophet, Samuel, had anointed David to be the next king of Israel and this had led to enmity between Saul and David. It was appreciated that David had respected the fact that Saul was currently the anointed king of Israel and thus, on two occasions, had refused to kill Saul in his sleep. These opportunities had arisen when David had found Saul inadequately guarded at a time when Saul was with his army, attempting to seek out David to kill him. To Benaiah, here was a hero on whom to model his own life. This feeling was strengthened by what happened as the forces reunited at the Besor Ravine.

The two-hundred men who had guarded the supplies at the Besor Ravine came out to meet David's victorious army, amazed at the vast amount of recovered plunder they brought with them. This wasn't just the plunder the Amalekites had taken when they overran Ziklag. The Amalekites had been marauding the Negev for years and had acquired a huge amount of booty. Initially, the men who had remained behind were delighted to be reunited with their wives and children who were all in good spirits and unharmed, but then a contentious issue arose. A few troublemakers among the four hundred who had gone to battle with the Amalekites claimed that all the booty was theirs. The two hundred who had remained behind had not faced the danger of battle and should just be content with having the womenfolk and children restored. News of this issue reached David's ears and he summoned the whole army to assemble, those who had fought and those who had guarded the baggage so he could address them.

David climbed onto a makeshift platform which had been constructed from some of the boxes of plunder recovered from the Amalekites.

"Men of Israel," he began, "the Lord has wonderfully answered our prayers. He guided us as we pursued the Amalekites. He provided the Egyptian guide to show us the way to follow when we had lost the trail. He gave us a glorious victory. He has restored to us our wives and children. Lest any think we have done all this by our own ability and strength, listen to my words. The Lord has done this for us. We have recovered more than we had lost. We have brought back wealth beyond anything we could have imagined. Therefore, we will share and share alike. Those who guarded the baggage will take as large a portion as those who did the fighting. We are Israelites. We must live as a united people and not allow greed and selfishness to break our unity. To God, the Lord of Hosts, be the glory. Yes, our God, the God of Abraham, Isaac and Jacob, to him be the glory. We are his servants and as his people, we must be as generous as he is with us. Yes, again I say, to God be the Glory." [9]

David spoke his closing words with a great crescendo and all the men, including those who had first sown the dissension, burst into rapturous cheering and applause. Benaiah joined in with this acclamation thinking what a supreme hero and leader was David, this great King of Israel in waiting. What a privilege it would be to serve him. What Benaiah learned from the other soldiers and what happened when they finally returned to Ziklag caused Benaiah to somewhat revise his opinion of David.

It appeared that David had been in the service of Israel's arch enemy, Achish, king of the Philistines. Achish had awarded Ziklag, which had formerly been a Philistine settlement, to David in view of the faithful service he had rendered. The only reason that David had not gone with Achish to fight Saul's army was the fact that Achish's other commanders did not trust David. They expected that he would change sides when confronted with an army from his own people. Achish, on the other hand, considered that David would have been trusted to fight against the Israelites because David had reported to Achish that he was destroying and plundering Israelite settlements when he and his soldiers were out foraging. Thus, Achish considered that David had made himself obnoxious to the Israelites and would not be able to desert him to re-join the Israelite ranks. David had in fact lied to Achish. In reality, he had only plundered the towns of tribes hostile to Israel and had massacred their inhabitants to avoid Achish hearing the truth.[10]

The army finally returned to Ziklag and were received with great rejoicing by those who had had to wait anxiously behind. None were more relieved than Jerusha and Acsah to be reunited with their menfolk, their husbands and especially the sons they had thought too young to go to battle. The two families soon felt fully integrated into the Israelite community in Ziklag and made a number of great friends. Abishag's particular friends were two girls of roughly the same age as herself, Rephalah and Shua. Her friendship with these girls was to become increasingly important to them as David consolidated his kingdom and his lifestyle became more that of an oriental potentate than a tribal chieftain, fighting to maintain his people's security in a hostile environment.

The victorious army had returned with far more spoil than the settlement at Ziklag could comfortably accommodate. The livestock alone couldn't be fed from the sparse pasture around Ziklag. Therefore, David arranged to distribute the excess wealth among the Israelite towns which had helped and supported him over the time he had been a fugitive from Saul. This was a politically wise move.[11]

Three days after David had returned to Ziklag, a travelworn person from Saul's army arrived at the settlement with news of the battle at Gilboa which went beyond the limited account that Jehoiada and Elhanan had been able to give on their earlier arrival at Ziklag.

Yes, the Philistines had annihilated the Israelite army. Jonathan had been killed and Saul had committed suicide. The soldier claimed that he had assisted Saul in his suicide. This was unlikely but knowing that enmity existed between Saul and David, the soldier thought that this claim might curry favour with the new king. How wrong he was. David was most upset. In spite of the enmity between them, David respected Saul as the great warrior king that he was, and Jonathan was his particular friend.

David's immediate reaction to receiving the news was to lead the court into a time of mourning. That evening, David recalled the soldier who had brought the news of Saul's death and made further enquiries. The soldier explained that he was an Amalekite. In view of what had just taken place at Ziklag, the Amalekites were not flavour of the month. Indeed, they had never been. The Amalekites were the earliest tribe to have shown hostility towards the Israelites, confronting them in battle at a place in Sinai called Rephidim.[70] This battle had taken place not that long after the Israelites had crossed the Red Sea and were on their journey from

Egypt to Canaan. However, in order to have been accepted into the Israelite army, this Amalekite must have rejected the idolatrous faith of his nation and accepted the Lord, Jehovah, as his God. Being an Amalekite by race shouldn't have therefore counted against him. During his career in the Israelite army, Benaiah was to meet a number of prominent men at arms who had rejected their own faith, replacing this by faith in the all-powerful God of the Israelites. Among these were Uriah, the Hittite, Ittai, a Philistine from Gath, and Zelek, an Ammonite, each of them becoming in due course, respected warriors in David's army.

David challenged this Amalekite on how he could have dared to have been involved in the killing of an anointed king. David obviously regarded the death of Saul as an act of regicide. He ordered that the Amalekite should be executed on the spot.[12] Benaiah, and indeed the rest of the family, privately regarded this as a totally unjust act but dared not publicly voice an opinion which might have been regarded as showing hostility to David.

Chapter 4

Consolidation of David's Kingdom

Now that Saul was dead and it was widely known that Samuel had anointed David as King of Israel, the nation should have immediately united under his leadership. However, following situations of near civil war, political matters are rarely sorted out in a simple and straightforward way. David moved from Ziklag to Hebron and was ceremonially re-anointed as King by the tribe of Judah. During his time at Hebron, David married more wives by whom he had a number of sons. It is important to note the names of the eldest sons, for at the time, it may have seemed likely that one of these would succeed David to the throne. The eldest was Amnon, son of Ahinoam, then Kileab, son of Abigail. His third son by Maacah was Absalom and Adonijah, son of Haggith, was his fourth son.[13]

Saul's general, Abner, who had escaped from Gilboa, took Saul's eldest surviving son, Ishbosheph, and declared him as king over the northern tribes of Israel. Although David had been anointed king by Samuel, Saul had been a Benjaminite and this tribe was not immediately prepared to accept a king over them from a southern tribe. Thus, hostility existed between Judah in the south and the northern tribes. Frequent skirmishes took place between the men of Judah and the northern tribesmen. A meeting was arranged between Joab and Abner, the generals of the armies from each side, to try to come to a permanent settlement. The two delegations negotiated from the opposite sides of the Pool of Gibeon. Rather than immediately going into a full-scale battle, an attempt was made to settle the issue by arranging for twelve men from each side to fight it out. This proved unsuccessful when they all ended up killing each other. The main army of Judah then launched an attack on the army of Israel and defeated them. Abner and the remnants of his army scattered and fled, pursued by the men of Judah.[14]

Abner found himself being chased by Joab's brother, Asahel. Abner was the more experienced warrior of the two and he knew he would defeat Asahel in a fight. However, not wishing to create a blood feud with Joab by killing Asahel, Abner tried to persuade Asahel to pursue a different prey. Asahel refused to give up the pursuit. Unbeknown to Asahel, Abner's spear was sharpened at each end, the butt as well as the metal point fixed to the top of the spear. As Asahel rushed after Abner, Abner suddenly stopped and raised the end of his spear so that Asahel became impaled on the sharp butt end of the spear and Asahel died instantly.[15]

As the sun started to set, Abner and his remaining soldiers formed into a group behind Abner and Abner called out to Joab, still in pursuit, and negotiated a truce. And thus, the two sides separated without the problem being resolved.[16]

A dispute then arose between Abner and Ishbosheph. The outcome of this dispute did lead to the resolution of the problem existing between the tribes of Judah and Benjamin but in a very unpleasant way.

It was common practice in those ancient kingdoms for the successor of a king to take over his harem to indicate that he was the one now in control. Now Saul had a very beautiful wife called Rizpah and after Saul died, Abner married her. As Abner was Saul's cousin, he may have been seen to have a claim to Saul's throne himself. Ishbosheph therefore interpreted this marriage as a provocative act on Abner's part and took him to task.

"Whatever do you think you're doing?" he challenged Abner. "Do you think that by marrying my father's wife, you'll convince Israel that you're really the one in charge and therefore should be king in my place?"

"Don't be so ridiculous, Ishbosheph. Had I really wanted to be king, I'd never have had you proclaimed king in the first place. As commander of the army, there is little you could have done to stop me from declaring myself as king. Even now, your position as king is entirely dependent on my support."

"Commander of the army!" retorted Ishbosheph. "A fine commander you've turned out to be. On two occasions during hostilities with David, you failed to provide an adequate guard to protect my father. He could then so easily have been killed by David when he found him unguarded and asleep. You deserted him at Gilboa and left him to be killed by the Philistines. Don't come the 'I'm a great army commander' with me, Abner!"

Abner took great offence at these words.

"I didn't desert your father at Gilboa. You don't know how the battle planned out. You weren't there. Saul left you behind when he went on that campaign because you were the most incompetent officer in your father's army. At Gilboa, the battle went in such a way that the Philistines were able to separate the two parts of our army. Saul's part was surrounded and annihilated. My part of the army was able to fight its way out. Don't accuse me of being a deserter."

The relationship between Abner and Ishbosheph became increasingly bitter. In the end, Abner decided that he could no longer support Ishbosheph and he sent a letter to David stating that he would come over to David's side and would bring the allegiance of Israel with him. David accepted Abner's offer on condition that he would bring to him, Michal, daughter of Saul, his first wife. David had, after all, been required to kill a hundred Philistines as the price for being allowed to become betrothed to Michal. When David became alienated from Saul, Saul arranged for Michal to marry someone else, a man called Paltiel. Michal was now very happily married to Paltiel but in order to complete the bargain, she was forcibly taken from Paltiel and restored to David, much to the dismay of Michal and Paltiel.[17]

A situation now existed which precipitated two grisly murders.

Joab murdered Abner, fearful that he might replace him as army commander. He used the excuse that Abner had killed his brother, Asahel, and Abner had to be killed in turn to settle the blood feud which now existed.[18]

Two of Ishbosheph's servants, Baanah and Recab, a pair of brothers, were really up to no good. They believed that they would curry favour with David if they killed Ishbosheph, the only obstacle between David and his becoming king of all Israel. They clearly didn't know what David's reaction had been when the Amalekite had reported that he had had a hand in Saul's death at Gilboa. They murdered Ishbosheph in his sleep and took his head to David.

David was furious at both murders. Joab as army commander was in an unassailable position but Baanah and Recab had miscalculated David's reaction and he had them executed. While David himself could do nothing to avenge the death of Abner, he expressed a hope that in due course, the Lord would repay Joab for that evil deed.[19]

So it was, all the tribes of Israel came to Hebron which David had made his capital and they declared David to be king over all Israel.

An incident which occurred fairly early in the reign of David, brought Benaiah and Zalmon to his attention as young men of valour with great potential as soldiers in his army. It occurred at a time when the Philistines had taken control of David's home city of Bethlehem. Abishai, Joab's brother, was a highly respected commander in David's army. One day, he overheard

David bemoaning the fact that the town where he had been born was now in Philistine control.

"I'm bitterly distressed," lamented David. "The Philistines have taken over Bethlehem, my birthplace. How I wish that someone would get me a drink of water from the well just outside the gate of that city."

It wasn't that David was short of water. His yearning was not so much for a drink but for Bethlehem to come back into Israelite control.

Abishai looked round for two young men, hungry for glory and noted Benaiah and Zalmon who had acquitted themselves so well in the military engagements in which they'd been involved.

"The king wants a drink of water from the well by the Gates of Bethlehem," he called out to Benaiah and Zalmon. "Come with me and we'll get him just that."

Benaiah and Zalmon enthusiastically responded and gathered their weapons and armour as they joined Abishai to embark on this highly dangerous venture. As they got close to Bethlehem, they stealthily made their way, taking cover to remain out of sight until they could peer through the shelter of a bush just a few yards from the well. They took stock of the situation. Half a dozen Philistine soldiers were on guard at the gate. They were clearly in a relaxed mood and quite unaware of the proximity of Abishai and his two men at arms.

"We'll need to engage them when they look as if they least expect an attack," Abishai stated in hushed tone. "I'll watch for the right opportunity and when I shout 'NOW!', we'll rush them."

Several minutes passed. The three Israelites waited in breathless anticipation, not daring to give away their whereabouts at this point. Two of the Philistines ambled back through the city gates and two of the others sat down, laying aside their weapons.

"NOW!" came Abishai's command and the three of them rushed out of hiding and were upon the Philistines who had barely time to pick up their weapons. Abishai struck one of them down, Benaiah struck such a mighty blow on the sword which his Philistine opponent held to protect himself that it flew out of his hand. Benaiah then immediately ran him through. Abishai and Benaiah engaged the two remaining Philistines while Zalmon carried out his task of filling a flask with water from the Bethlehem well. After a very few minutes which was all it took to draw the water, Zalmon shouted,

"Flask full!"

Abishai and Benaiah disengaged from their startled and shocked antagonists, ran from the scene and made their way back to David. They followed a route across hard ground where it was unlikely that any trail left could be identified and followed. The whole engagement at Bethlehem had barely lasted more than a quarter of an hour.

When they returned, David was extremely moved by the gallantry of these three.

"I can't drink this water," he declared "for that would be like drinking the blood of my gallant soldiers."[20]

David assembled the army and stood on a platform to address them. He called on Abishai, Benaiah and Zalmon to stand by him.

"Three of your number have exhibited the daring and gallantry which is so characteristic of you all, my beloved and valiant soldiers," he started. "On hearing me express a wish to drink from the water from the well by the gate of my beloved city and birthplace, these three, Abishai, Benaiah and Zalmon, set out for Bethlehem to retrieve for me just that, a flask of water from the well at Bethlehem in spite of it now being under the control of the Philistines. They smote the Philistines guarding the well and have brought back to me this flask of Bethlehem well water."

David held aloft the precious flask.

"Much as I would like to, I can't drink this water for to me, it represents what could have been the shed blood of my own men, so gallantly risked to meet my least desire. Instead, I will scatter this water upon you, my loyal subjects, that this may be a symbolic anointing of you with the courage and daring which marks you all out as very special men."

With that, David poured out water from the flask held in his left hand on to his right hand and splashed this across the assembled troops. The soldiers responded with a spontaneous cheer before being stood down by their officers.

Not everyone was pleased with what had happened. Jerusha and Acsah were very angry that Abishai had recruited such young soldiers to accompany him on what at the outset, might have appeared to be a suicide mission. Abishag on the other hand was rather proud of the courage displayed by Benaiah, the young man of whom she had become so fond.

Chapter 5

Jerusalem

David ruled Israel from Hebron for seven years. During this time, Benaiah and Zalmon grew from boyhood to manhood and became trained in the art of warfare as they accompanied the army in their forays into the surrounding countryside to reconnoitre the land. They distinguished themselves well in the skirmishes which arose as they encroached land which other tribes regarded as their territory. A nearby town which became a particular focus of David's interest was Jebus, a fortress city set on a hill. Its position seemed to make it virtually impregnable and the Jebusites boasted that it could be held against any invader by the blind and the lame.

David recognised the strategic value that occupying this city would represent for any seeking to control all the surrounding countryside, but how could it be taken. The city had one weakness, the tunnel which led to its water supply. Any attempt to take the city through this tunnel would be a risky business as only three men at a time could emerge abreast from the tunnel to take on the Jebusites. However, Joab took some of his best soldiers through this tunnel and managed to establish a bridgehead at the end of the tunnel enabling more soldiers to join him. From this bridgehead, the army fanned out and took the rest of the city.[21]

David moved from Hebron to Jebus and established this as his new capital. He renamed Jebus, Jerusalem, meaning 'Foundation of Peace' but it has been referred to by other names over the years; 'David's City', 'the Holy City' and 'Zion'.

As David settled into the city, he realised that improvements in the buildings were needed but the Israelites were a nation of farmers and warriors and didn't have a tradition of constructing fine buildings. He started negotiations with Hiram, the King of Tyre. Tyre was well to the north of the land which the Israelites sought to claim as their sovereign territory. David entered into a trading arrangement by which Hiram supplied David with wood from his extensive cedar forests and a team of skilled craftsmen, mainly carpenters and stone masons, who could oversee building work. One of their first projects was the construction of a magnificent palace for David.[22] This was an impressive building. It was entered through an imposing portico which led to a large inner court around which were grouped functional buildings, a banqueting hall, comfortable living accommodation for David and his wives, a throne room and quarters for senior palace servants. Beyond these were smaller courtyards around which were grouped buildings in which the junior, domestic servants lived and where kitchens, laundries and an armoury were located. This project took many years to complete.

As David started to settle into the comforts of life in this big city, he married more wives and took in women who were not regarded as wives but had the lesser status of concubines.[23] This was common practice among oriental potentates. He appointed one of his official wives, Eglah, to not only take charge of his harem of concubines but to seek out other pretty Israelite girls to add to this harem. While the comfortable lifestyle afforded by becoming a concubine suited the more languid type of girl, most of the Israelite girls dreaded the loss of freedom that would be involved if Eglah were to identify them as suitable to become one of David's concubines.

Concern was felt in the households of Jehoiada and Elhanan. They disapproved of David's marital arrangements. This topic arose when they met to discuss matters of interest.

"I think the teaching we have from the history of our people makes it clear that monogamy is the preferred rule for society to follow," pontificated Jehoiada.

"Many of the tribes which we've had to contend with in establishing our right to settle in this land are descendants of Abraham's polygamous relationships. Our four times married forefather, Israel, had a dysfunctional family which he couldn't control. His sons, including our ancestor, Judah, performed all sorts of misdeeds. David has no need to establish a harem to be like other kings around. As king of God's people, he should be prepared to be different and pay more attention to what can be discerned as God's way of working."

Elhanan agreed but added, "It must be said in mitigation to Jacob that he was tricked by his uncle, Laban, into marrying both his daughters while it was clear that Jacob would have been content to marry just Rachel."[127]

Elhanan had a further cause for concern. His daughter, Abishag, was growing into a very beautiful woman and he was worried that she might come to the attention of Eglah. Although she was still only a teenager, this was not a disqualification which would have spared her being conscripted into David's harem. The qualification for becoming a member of the harem was that the girl had to be a virgin on entering into this form of service to David, and Abishag certainly was that.

A solution which would have avoided Abishag being recruited as a member of David's harem came up as they continued their discussion. They had noticed how strongly Benaiah and Abishag were attracted to one another. Although too young for marriage, there was no reason why these two young people should not become betrothed if they were both agreeable to the idea. The suggestion was made to the two young people separately and they both readily agreed. Benaiah added the caution that he felt it would be wrong to actually marry before he had fulfilled his obligation to serve in the army and was released from military service. He had seen too many of his friends' wives left as grieving widows when their husbands had been killed in battle and he wanted to spare Abishag this sadness. And so it was that Benaiah and Abishag became betrothed. They followed the custom of the day which involved the bridegroom giving the bride-to-be a gift. The gift, as today, was usually a ring but this was placed, not on the third finger, but on the bride's index finger. The gift was made ceremoniously, Benaiah reciting the line traditionally used at betrothal ceremonies,

"Be thou consecrated unto me according to the law of Moses and Israel by means of this ring."

It was unusual to restrict the betrothal gift just to a ring and additional gifts were often included too. In view of the reason for the long delay before the actual wedding could take place, Benaiah gave Abishag a small, replica shield cast in bronze. This shield was only the size of an ornament, not something which would afford any protection in a battle, but it was there to remind Abishag that Benaiah would need protection when away fighting battles. What better protection could there be than Abishag's prayers.

The betrothal safeguarded Abishag from being conscripted into David's harem. Even in that society where serving God and observing his standards should have been considered a priority of life, becoming betrothed often signified that the girl was no longer a virgin.

The fact that David was now well established as king of Israel and had taken an impregnable city as his capital was a matter of great concern for the Philistines, the nation with whom Israel most fiercely contested control over the land. The Philistines decided to make a supreme effort to rid the land of David. The Philistine army came and camped in the Valley of Rephaim. David was aware that his predecessor, Saul, had made mistakes by not adequately seeking God's guidance when making military decisions so he had wisely established a team of advisers to guide him in his decision making. These included Joab, the general of his army, Zadok and Ahimelech, the chief priests, Nathan, the prophet, and two men, noted for their wisdom, Ahithophel and Hushai. David's eldest sons were also invited to meet with this panel of advisers. A learned scribe, Seraiah was appointed as secretary to keep notes of proceedings and record the decisions made.[24] These advisers met to determine what response should be made to this act of aggression by the Philistines. There were two possible courses of action. Either they could either remain in the safety of Jerusalem and wait for the Philistines to come and attack the city or go out and meet the Philistines in battle. They prayed and received a clear answer that if they went out to do battle with the Philistines, God would give them victory.

So it was, David's army went out to fight the Philistines and defeated them. There were casualties on David's side. In particular, Makir, the leader of the Kerethites and Pelethites, an elite regiment in the army and designated 'the King's Bodyguard', had been killed. Witnessing the death of their leader during the battle, Benaiah, who fought in the ranks of this regiment, had taken over command. He was a natural leader and the regiment inflicted great losses on the Philistines as the battle proceeded. Benaiah's act of leadership came to David's attention. Benaiah was known to be a very able and courageous young soldier who had achieved promotion to a fairly senior rank in the army at an absurdly young age. At the end of the battle, David confirmed Benaiah as the new leader of the Kerethites and Pelethites and invited him to become part of his council of advisers.[24]

The army returned to Jerusalem in a state of euphoria, bringing with them the Philistine idols which had been left behind as the Philistines fled from the field. The euphoria was only short lived. News came back to Jerusalem that the Philistines who had been forced to retreat from the battle had done so in relatively good order without receiving too many casualties. They had reassembled in the Valley of Rephaim with reinforcements and looked set to fight again. David reconvened his council which this time included Benaiah.

"Should they go out and fight as before?"

Benaiah sounded a word of caution :-

"The Philistines have observed our battle tactics. It would be a mistake for us to go out and fight in exactly the same way. They'll be prepared. I noticed that there was a fairly thick forest of balsam trees behind the Philistine lines into which they were able to retreat when they saw the battle had been lost. I would suggest that we send a relatively small contingent to take up battle positions as before in front of the Philistine army but that our main force should circle round behind the balsam trees. When the main army is ready, the force in front of the Philistines should launch an attack but this will be a decoy. As the Philistines advance to meet the decoy attack, the main army should burst through the balsam trees and attack the Philistines from the rear."

This sounded a good plan of action but again, they needed to pray. At the end of the time of prayer they waited to see what answer God might give. Nathan the prophet stepped forward :-

"The Lord has indicated to me that Benaiah's plan is a good one. However, you will need a sign from the Lord to let the two parts of the army know when is the right moment to attack. You will hear the sound of marching feet above the balsam trees. This will be the heavenly army of the Lord of hosts. At this sound, move into attack for that sign will mean that the Lord has gone before you."

The Israelites went out to attack, but this time, following the plan which had been endorsed by God. The sound of marching feet above the balsam trees signalled the time to start the engagement. Benaiah had the dangerous job of commanding the smaller Israelite force which was a decoy and would be the first to launch the attack on the Philistine army.

The plan worked to perfection. This time the Philistines were comprehensively defeated and the Israelites did not give them time to regroup. Instead of immediately returning to Jerusalem, they pursued the Philistines, harrying them until they were back in their own territory. David renamed the site where the battle had been fought, 'Baal Perazim' meaning 'the Lord has broken out against his enemies and their gods'.[25]

So life was able to continue in peace and security in Jerusalem. Nathan the prophet came to David and indicated to David that Jerusalem should not just be the political capital of Israel but it should also be its religious heart. In order for this to come about, the Ark of the Covenant should be located in the city. This suggestion seemed good to David.

Some years earlier, the Ark had been captured by the Philistines in the days when Eli was High Priest at the battle of Ebenezer.[26] However, the presence of the Ark in Philistine territory had brought a series of calamities on the Philistines[27] and they were glad to return it. It was currently kept at the house of an Israelite named Abinadab.[28] David and his bodyguard, the Kerethites and Pelethites, now under the command of Benaiah, and supported by other specially selected army units, marched out to the home of Abinadab to escort the Ark back to Jerusalem. The force numbered about thirty thousand men.[29] However, the return journey was not without incident.

The ox cart on which the Ark was carried was accompanied by Abinadab's sons, Uzzah and Ahio. When they came to a farm at a place called Nacon, the ground was particularly rutted and uneven. The oxen started to stumble and the Ark was shaken about on the cart. It hadn't been properly secured. Uzzah began to curse and swear and roughly pulled the Ark back into the middle of the ox cart. Although the sky was cloudless, there came a sound like a clap of thunder and Uzzah dropped down, dead on the spot. The procession stopped. An awed silence fell upon those escorting the Ark. David felt very angry and upset because he thought that this was a sign from God that the Ark should not proceed to Jerusalem. He made the decision to store the Ark at the home of Obed-Edom who was not an ethnic Israelite but a Gittite who had converted to worship Jehovah, the God of Israel. David returned with the escort to Jerusalem and await guidance from God. Everyone was feeling very depressed.[30]

This setback weighed heavily on David's mind for about three months. He went to Nathan to seek guidance about what steps he should now take regarding the Ark. Nathan explained to David that the death of Uzzah was not a sign of divine displeasure against David but against Uzzah alone. The Ark was a most holy item and needed to be treated with the reverence due. This reverence had not been forthcoming at the home of Abinadab. Uzzah's contemptuous action in grabbing the Ark as if it were a nuisance item was the last straw and earned him divine retribution. Nathan pointed out that the Ark had been respected while at the home of Obed-Edom but had been neglected at the house of Abinadab. As a result, the household of Obed-Edom had been richly blessed while the Ark resided at this home but Abinadab's household had missed out on these blessings.

David realised that the way was therefore clear to resume the process of bringing the Ark to Jerusalem. This time, special steps were taken to ensure the Ark was treated with due respect. Those who had the privilege of carrying the Ark underwent ritual purification first before handling the Ark. The Ark finally arrived in Jerusalem amid great rejoicing. David led the celebrations, enthusiastically dancing ahead of the procession without inhibition or restraint.[31] The people went wild with enthusiasm and imitated David's exuberance. This holy and significant item was going to be placed at the heart of the emergent nation of Israel. The Ark was set in place in a tabernacle, a tent which David had had set up. He had followed the design instructions which had been given to Moses who constructed the first tabernacle during the wilderness wonderings of the Israelites, departing Egypt.[32]

Sadly, the joyful day ended on a sour note. David's wife, Michal, Saul's daughter, had disdainfully watched the celebration from a palace window and she was not impressed. Michal was in a disgruntled mood. She hadn't been happy about being separated from a husband she loved to be restored to David for no better reason than to satisfy David's pride. She hadn't even been accorded the honour of being his prime wife but was just another woman among David's many wives and concubines. David had shown scant gratitude to Michal many years earlier when she had risked her own life to enable him to escape from Saul and in those days, she really loved David.

When David returned to the palace, Michal vented her disgust.

"I was ashamed of you," she spat out as she came into his presence. "You danced and cavorted like a man who had utterly lost his self-control. What a ridiculous spectacle you created for the servant and slave girls by your vulgar display. I'm a king's daughter and my father, Saul, would never have behaved in so disgusting a manner. Now I'm a king's wife, I expect my husband to behave like a king."

David was absolutely astonished and dismayed by his wife's attitude.

"What you despise, Michal, was a genuine act of unrestrained worship of the Lord, something your father was never able to do. I don't mind seeming undignified. I'm more than prepared to humiliate myself if this brings glory to God. Far from being despised by the slave girls and servants whom you hold in such low esteem, I was honoured in their eyes because everything I did was an act of uninhibited worship to the Lord."

In great anger, David banished Michal from his sight to another part of the palace and he never saw her again![33]

David's thoughts often rested on the Ark and the way it was sheltered, not in a proper building, but in the tabernacle. This was really, no more than a tent, even though it had been erected following the precise details which God had revealed to Moses. A portable tent was appropriate to accommodate this holy object while it was being transported, initially through Sinai where the Israelites journeyed as nomads, and more recently, around the land which God had given to the Israelites. However, a more durable building was now needed. David therefore consulted Nathan, suggesting that the Ark, representing the presence of God, should be located in a building, at least as splendid as the palace he himself now occupied. David told Nathan that he had in mind to build a temple as a beautiful edifice, fit to be the resting place for something as important and holy as the Ark.[34]

Nathan initially agreed that this would indeed be a good idea but when Nathan returned home and prayed about the matter, God told Nathan that he would build a house for David (meaning creating a dynasty of kings descended from David rather than an actual building). However, the construction of a house in which the Ark of the Covenant was to be located, should be a task carried out by one of David's direct descendants rather than by the warrior king, David himself. God wished to be revered as a god of peace and not as a god associated with conquest and violence. Nathan passed this message on to David and the Temple building project was therefore shelved for a generation.[35]

Chapter 6

Benaiah's Prowess

By now, the tribes of Israel were in control of most of the territory which had been defined to Moses as the land they would possess in perpetuity. However, Israel still felt under threat from neighbouring tribes in and around this land. David sought to consolidate his kingdom by defeating these tribes which he considered undermined the security of his kingdom. Benaiah's valour and conspicuous bravery during the campaigns against these hostile tribes marked him out as a truly exceptional warrior.

Although comprehensively defeated at Baal Perazim, the Philistines remained a threat to the kingdom and David defeated them again at Metheg Ammah. Benaiah played a prominent part in achieving this victory which gave Israel unchallenged dominance over the Philistines.

David next turned his attention to the Moabites who occupied land to the east of the Salt Sea (Dead Sea) but who frequently sent raiding parties across the river Jordan to plunder Israelite settlements. When the Israelite and Moabite armies confronted each other, things initially went badly for the Israelites. It was clear that the Moabites were led by two exceptional warriors who were able to lead their men deep into the Israelite army, cutting swathes through the Israelite forces. Sections of the Israelite army were being left isolated and outnumbered by the men of Moab. Benaiah was called upon to lead his men into conflict with the parts of the Moabite army led by these warriors who were fighting the Israelites with devastating efficiency. These two leading Moabite warriors were easy to identify in the fray and Benaiah fought his way through to confront first one and then the other of these warriors in single combat.[36] For a moment, as each of these fights took place, the forces of the two armies close to these one on one battles drew back to witness the epic encounters taking place. The combats were hard fought, but in each case, Benaiah emerged victorious. Although wounded in these encounters, Benaiah continued to lead his men. With the loss of their illustrious heroes, the Moabites were soon defeated.

At the end of the battle, David carried out an act which Benaiah found most distasteful and unnecessary. He lined up the prisoners of war and executed two-thirds of them.[37] From a strategic standpoint, this meant that the Moabites fighting strength was so weakened that they would never again be a threat to David. Thus, the Moabites became David's tributaries.

David next turned his attention to the Arameans who fought under Hadadezer, king of Zobah. A huge battle was fought in which the Arameans lost twenty-two thousand men. David took seven thousand charioteers and twenty thousand foot soldiers as prisoners of war and captured a thousand chariots. Having recovered from his wounds, Benaiah had again performed with conspicuous gallantry in this battle, leading his regiment to inflict heavy casualties on the Arameans in the areas of battle where they appeared to be the most dangerous. David passed through the Aramean kingdom, which roughly corresponds to the country we now call Syria, taking an immense amount of booty. He set up a garrison in their main city, Damascus, and like the Moabites, the Arameans became David's tributaries.

David then moved south of Moab to Edom to subdue this nation. For years, the Edomites, no less than the Moabites, had been a thorn in the flesh of the Israelites who had settled in the south. They frequently raided and pillaged their villages. The Edomites had a number of Egyptian mercenaries in their army, including a veritable giant of a man. The two forces met for battle in the Valley of Salt. Benaiah marked out the Egyptian as the most dangerous soldier in the Edomite army and made his way though the battle lines to confront him. The Egyptian was armed with a huge spear. Benaiah had selected a heavy club as his weapon to fight this man. Benaiah was able to evade the Egyptians spear thrusts but the Egyptian was able to use his spear to dislodge the warclub from Benaiah's hands. Benaiah darted to get inside the range of the pointed end of the spear, grabbed the spear and attempted to take the spear from the Egyptian. The Egyptian was very much bigger than Benaiah and it looked unlikely that Benaiah would succeed. However, Benaiah did manage to wrench the spear from the Egyptian who stumbled and fell as Benaiah jerked the spear from him. Benaiah immediately killed the Egyptian with his own spear.[38] This encounter had been Benaiah's most challenging fight to date and his victory left Benaiah with a great sense of exhilaration. The battle continued in Israel's favour and with the victory won, David set up garrisons throughout Edom. Thus, the Edomites became his subjects.

Further campaigns were fought to subdue the Amalekites and the Ammonites. However, the Ammonites were not completely defeated and remained a threat to be dealt with later. Winter was approaching and the army made its way home.

On this return journey, Benaiah was called upon to use his valour in a civilian cause. With all forms of danger apparently behind them, rather than set up a camp protected by a ring of sentries for the night, the army was given a few days leave and separated to billet in the homes of nearby Israelite villages. The soldiers were relieved to be able to sleep with a roof over their heads rather than in a draughty tent. The home where Benaiah was billeted told him that they were being plagued by a lion whose lair was somewhere in the nearby hills and was killing cattle and sheep from among their flocks. It was a dangerous beast and they were unable to corner it.

Benaiah asked his hosts to gather together the villagers to talk about the issue and more importantly, to pray that this scourge might be removed. Benaiah was taking a leaf from David's book whom he'd observed always took time to pray before embarking on a battle. The villagers were somewhat negative about their chances of removing the lion. Those who had seen him described how fierce and strong he was. The atmosphere seemed more positive after the prayer time. Benaiah undertook to seek out and destroy this lion the following morning. This was much to the gratitude of the villagers.

Benaiah felt a little uneasy about this mission. He was trained and skilled in confronting human adversaries on the battlefield but he'd never before had to deal with a powerful and dangerous wild animal. One of the problems which crossed Benaiah's mind was the need to actually locate the lion. Wherever would he find this beast whose lair could have been anywhere in the hills some distance from the fields where the villagers pastured their flocks? The time of prayer had eased Benaiah's mind every bit as much as it had the villagers and Benaiah slept soundly that night. He awoke next morning to discover that part of his prayer had been answered. There had been a freak snowfall overnight which would make it easier to track the lion. A snowfall at this altitude in that land was a very rare event and many of the villagers had never before seen snow!

Benaiah, armed with his spear and a sharp hunting knife, set out on his quest. It didn't take too long to pick up the lion's trail. It's large footprints were clear to follow in the newly fallen snow. The footprints led to a deep pit and Benaiah realised that the lion's lair lay somewhere in the pit. Benaiah felt a tremble of excitement and anticipation. He would now need to tread cautiously. Where exactly was the lion holed up? He carefully made his way down the slope clasping his spear in one hand and the short but very sharp hunting knife held firmly in the other. No sooner was he at the bottom of the pit than the lion was on him, springing out from behind a bush. The lion fell on top of Benaiah, knocking the spear out of his hand. Strangely, this close contact proved to be to Benaiah's advantage and saved his life. Benaiah immediately plunged his knife deep into the lion's throat. The lion gave a roar, blood spurted from the wound and it rolled over, dead.[39] The lion's claws had torn a deep gash into one of Benaiah's arms but his body had been largely protected by the armour he wore. Benaiah decapitated the lion and returned with this gory trophy to the village where he had lodged.

The villagers were ecstatic. The threat to their livelihood had been removed. The wounds the lion had inflicted on Benaiah's arms were not too serious and were carefully dressed. Benaiah was able to take a few days well-earned rest to nurse his wounds among these grateful villagers before his leave time had ended and he had to return to the army.

The victorious army at last reached Jerusalem and entered the city amid great acclaim. Its exploits and success had already been reported by messengers, sent on ahead. Benaiah's proud family were among the crowd, welcoming the returning troops. As soon as the parade dispersed, Benaiah, along with Jehoiada, Elhanan and Zalmon who had also performed valiantly during the recent campaigns, returned to their homes and their women folk. Jerusha, Acsah and Abishag had anxiously waited for their safe return during the time they had been away, fighting Israel's enemies. Benaiah sank into the arms of Abishag, his betrothed. She was weeping with joy at this reunion. At the same time, she was radiant with pride as Benaiah's exploits had already been recounted to her.

"I don't ever want you to encounter such danger again," she declared amid the sobs of relief at having her beloved safely back home.

In those days, medals were not presented to soldiers who had shown great valour. Instead of medals, a warrior's prowess could be measured by his war scars and Benaiah had certainly returned with those.

Chapter 7

Continuing war against the Ammonites

In the spring, the army was remobilised with a view to renewing hostilities against the Ammonites. The objective was to finally defeat the Ammonites and bring them into line with the other nations who had become allied to David. This time, David, who was now beginning to age, did not accompany the army which left Jerusalem under the command of Joab. Benaiah and the other members of his family who were soldiers, Jehoiada, Elhanan and Zalmon, were proud to be part of this army. Joab's army successfully drove the Ammonites back until their army was forced to take refuge in the city of Rabbah which was an Ammonite stronghold. During this period of siege, Joab sent one of Benaiah's fellow commanders, Uriah, the Hittite, back to Jerusalem to give David news of the campaign. A few days later, Uriah returned to his command having apparently fulfilled his mission.

Uriah, the Hittite, was an officer whom Benaiah knew well and particularly admired. He was honourable and courageous. The Hittites had occupied large parts of the land in which the Israelites were now settling, way back in the time of Abraham. Uriah told Benaiah that one of his ancestors, Ephron, had sold Abraham the land at Machpelah where he had buried his wife, Sarah[56]. Uriah continued to explain to Benaiah more about the Hittites.

"Most of my people have migrated to the north where they have built a great civilisation. However, some of us chose to remain in this land and identify with your people for your God, the God of Abraham, your ancestor, is a credible deity. He has displayed his power and revealed a code of laws which represent a sensible framework to regulate society. How different your God is from the impotent and worthless idols which the other tribes around us worship. They perpetuate some vile practices which sometimes even involve child sacrifice."

As the siege continued, Joab launched an attack with the objective of directly entering the city of Rabbah through its main gate. Benaiah was surprised to see Joab attempting this by adopting a means of assault which represented a very risky strategy. A seasoned campaigner like Joab should have known that attacking the city by attempting to break down its gates, defended by fortified towers, was unlikely to be successful. It would almost certainly result in heavy casualties being inflicted on the troops carrying out this order. However, Joab sent a contingent of soldiers under the leadership of Uriah to attack the main city gate and try to break through it. Uriah was a very valiant soldier. Whatever the danger, whatever the challenge, Uriah was up for it. Benaiah was amazed to see the courage and enthusiasm with which Uriah led his men to the Rabbah city gate in what was to prove a suicide mission.

The assault failed. Heavy casualties were taken as might have been expected. The troops around the gate, which was defended by fortified towers on each side, were vulnerable to attack from the defending Ammonites in these towers. Heavy objects were dropped on the assault force which was also being subjected to a continuous hail of arrows. When most of the force had been killed, including their captain, Uriah, the surviving soldiers fled from the danger zone, back to the lines of Israel's besieging army where they were located well out of range of the Ammonite archers. The result was not unexpected. Joab had apparently, disastrously failed to secure his objective.

Benaiah didn't discover an explanation for this rash manoeuvre, ordered by his general until he returned to Jerusalem. Jerusha, who had friends in the palace was able to recount what happened there. It would appear that David had committed adultery with Uriah's wife, Bathsheba, while Uriah was away with the army. When it was discovered that Bathsheba was pregnant, David had asked Joab to send Uriah back to Jerusalem, ostensibly to bring news of how the campaign was faring. David had expected Uriah to return to his home while in Jerusalem and sleep with his wife thinking that the child she bore would then appear to be Uriah's. However, out of loyalty to Joab and his fellow soldiers in the field who were suffering the deprivations of being on campaign, Uriah slept at the gates of David's palace with the soldiers who had been left there on guard.

When it was time for Uriah to return to the siege, he was sent with a sealed letter to Joab which asked Joab to place Uriah in the thickest of any battle being fought so that he stood a good chance of being killed. This then was the reason why Uriah had been sent to break through the city gates of Rabbah.[42]

Eyewitnesses at court had observed David's strange reactions to the news that a messenger from Joab brought of the heavy casualties that had been suffered by a contingent of soldiers, sent to break through the city gates. Initially, David was furious.

"Whatever does Joab think he's doing?" he exploded. "He knows very well from the history of our own warfare the folly of bringing soldiers too close to the walls of a city under attack."

David quoted the example of how one of the judges, Abimelech, had been killed when he took his men too close the city walls during the assault on the city of Thebes.[43]

After David's outburst, the messenger continued as Joab had instructed him by reporting that Uriah, the Hittite, was among those killed during this attempted assault on the city gate. A sudden transformation then took place in David's mood.

"Ah well," he said to the messenger, "These are the fortunes of war. Who can tell who the next casualty might be? When you return to Joab, tell him not to be discouraged by this setback but to continue with the siege. Press home the attack. I am confident that in due course, he will be able to destroy the city."[44]

After Bathsheba had completed the obligatory period of mourning for her late husband, Uriah, David had her brought to the palace where he made her his wife. In due course, she bore him a son. David hoped that this had brought an end to the matter, but it was not to be. David was to experience the Lord's displeasure at his having committed this shameful deed. He had murdered Uriah by arranging for him to be killed in what might have appeared to be the normal course of military conflict.[45]

Among David's advisers was the prophet, Nathan. He was fearless and outspoken. Nathan came to David and told him of a situation in which a rich man with large flocks had taken the only lamb possessed by a poor man to provide a meal to entertain a guest.

David's reaction to this story was one of great anger and he swore that this rich man should receive punishment for his evil deed.

"You are the man!" said Nathan in a quiet voice and waited to see David's reaction. David was stunned into silence.

Nathan continued, "In spite of all that God has done for you, all the wealth and success he has granted you, you have committed two of the worst sins possible, adultery and then compounded this by murder to cover your adultery. Because you killed Uriah with the sword of the Ammonites, violence will never leave your family. You will experience a series of calamities including seeing someone who is close to you and loved by you, publicly taking over your harem! You thought that you would be able to keep your sin secret, but the misfortunes which you will soon experience will be public knowledge throughout Israel."

David then started to express his contrition to Nathan and Nathan was able to tell David that this had ameliorated God's anger against David. David would not therefore experience the sudden death he deserved but the son which Bathsheba had borne him would die. As Nathan had prophesied, this son became ill.

David spent the next few days in extreme contrition, refusing the food the senior members of his household urged him to eat and prostrating himself on the ground in prayer. The child died seven days later and it was only then that David was prepared to break his fast.[44]

David comforted Bathsheba and in due course, she had another son whom they named Solomon. However, the prophet Nathan could see that this son was going to be specially loved by God and he knew the son, not by the name, Solomon, but by Jedediah meaning 'Loved by God'.[47]

Meanwhile, Joab was having great success in the battle to control Rabbah. He captured the citadel which protected the source of water for the city. He knew then that the city must therefore soon fall. He urged David to come with reinforcements to complete the job so that the honour of capturing the city would be David's. David arrived with the requested reinforcements and Rabbah fell. David plundered the city and moved on to take the rest of the Ammonite towns. David marked his victory by being crowned with the crown that had been worn by the king of the Ammonites. With the authority this represented, he was able to set the people to forced labour, making bricks and preparing the wood which would be needed as building materials to restore the towns and cities which had been devastated by David's armies during this war against the Ammonites.[48]

Chapter 8

Amnon and Tamar

A friendship had grown up between Nathan and Benaiah who had often found themselves on the same side when controversial issues were being discussed in the king's council. The king's domestic situation often cropped up in their course of their private discussion.

"How wise your parents have been to remain faithful to one another and avoid the practice of polygamy," remarked Nathan to Benaiah. "David has shown a significant lack of wisdom in this respect. He's no need of so many wives and a harem of concubines. I've lost count of the number of sons and daughters he's sired. They've become a burden on the royal exchequer."

"From what I see of the behaviour and attitudes of the king's sons, I can't help but feel that they'll be the source of misfortune to David which you prophesied would come about," observed Benaiah.

"You're surely right," agreed Nathan. "Whereas your parents were able to shower love on you and have succeeded in bringing you up, not just as a valiant soldier but as a man of honour, wisdom and integrity, David's sons are for the most part just spoiled brats.

David hasn't spent time with them, instructing them in the ways of the Lord as a good father should. He accedes to their every whim and doesn't correct them when they misbehave as they frequently do. Of the king's eldest sons, and one of these is the most likely to succeed him, Kileab seems to be the best of the bunch. Absalom has much going for him but he can be devious and is extreme in his actions when angered. Amnon and Adonijah however, seem to lack any sense of morality. Heaven forbid that either of these should become king.

Israel seems to have a tradition of having great leaders and patriarchs, but who have failed to be good fathers. Abraham and Jacob's family problems largely arose as a result of their being polygamous. Isaac only had one wife but even his family was dysfunctional and his sons fell out. Eli's sons were a disgrace and even the great priest and prophet, Samuel, couldn't control his sons."

Benaiah continued the conversation, making his own comments on David's marital arrangements.

"Abishag, who, as you know is my betrothed, has friends among the king's harem. They tell her that although they can have any material thing they ask for, good clothes, perfume, comfortable furniture, they find their lives to be utterly boring. They feel isolated in their suite of rooms and apartments in the palace complex with only one another for company. They are denied the friendship of men and are restricted in their freedom whenever they are able to venture out of the palace,"

Nathan frowned and shook his head.

"This is why polygamy is so wrong. It denigrates women in a harem to be no more than items for the king's pleasure. They're human beings, no less than the king, and should be given the same degree of human dignity but no, they're treated as no more than the king's chattels. His relationship with them is no more than physical and they're denied the opportunity to hold intelligent conversation with outsiders or to contribute to life around them in any other way but to satisfy David's lust. Indeed, with such a large harem, the opportunity for even this physical contact with David comes round but rarely."

"Is David really a fit person to be king of Israel?" Benaiah queried.

Nathan spoke in David's defence.

"It's true that he has been a disappointment in many ways but we all commit sins and David shows genuine remorse for his misdeeds. He does have a very real relationship with God and this is clearly shown in the beautiful psalms he's written to be used during our times of worship. His penitence is expressed in some of these. Yes, I could wish that David had done better and not committed such inexcusable sins but at present, there's no-one better to replace him from among David's household. I dread to think what might happen to the nation if one of his most spoilt sons becomes king."

Benaiah and Nathan parted and as they returned to their homes, Benaiah rejoiced that through Abishag being betrothed to himself, she was spared the tedium of living as a member of David's harem.

After a few years, David probably began to forget Nathan's prophecy, but the disasters Nathan had predicted suddenly came upon him and, as Benaiah had expected, they came through his sons.

David's second son was Kileab. He was son of Abigail, the widow of a very churlish man who had refused succour to David and his men when he was fleeing from Saul. Abigail had stepped in and her diplomacy avoided the bloodshed which may have otherwise ensued by ensuring that David and his men were supplied with the food they needed.[49] She was not only beautiful but a wise and intelligent woman and many considered that she was probably David's favourite wife. Kileab could have made a good king but he wasn't robust, frequently falling ill. Sadly, he contracted a fever and died while only in his late teens.

One day, soon after Kileab's death, the three Prince A's, Amnon, Absalom and Adonijah, found themselves alone together in the palace garden. Had any overheard their conversation, they would have realised the problems which were brewing within David's family.

There was a great rapport between Amnon and Adonijah but some hostility seemed to be directed towards Absalom.

Amnon started by directing his remarks to Absalom.

"I think your sister's trying to avoid me, Absalom. She could be doing herself a disfavour!"

"I don't think so. She's preserved her virginity so she's well away from you," replied Absalom.

"Oh, is Tamar a prude like her brother?" sneered Amnon.

"She's living according to the laws of Moses and following the best traditions of the people of Israel as well might you consider doing. Contrary to what you suggest, Tamar's doing herself a great favour by keeping out of your way," retorted Absalom.

Adonijah now entered the conversation.
"If she plays her cards right, Tamar could become Queen of Israel"

"To do that, she'd have to marry the King of Israel and I don't see either of you aspiring to that office," retorted Absalom.

Amnon bristled.
"I'm the eldest son. Of course, I'll be the next king,"

"David will choose his successor when the time is right and that's not now!" replied Absalom.

Adonijah interjected,
"I suppose you think that David might choose you to succeed him, Absalom, because you're daddy's favourite. Well it doesn't work like that. Succession goes to the eldest son unless there is some good reason why this shouldn't happen."

"Huh," a half laugh came from Absalom as he responded. "The way you two womanisers go round seducing virgins is more than good enough reason why neither of you is fit to be king."

"So goody, goody Absalom has just one wife," scoffed Adonijah. "You don't know what you're missing. I took Meriabah to bed last night. My word, she was a good lie. "

"I've had her too," injected Amnon to the conservation. "Yes, she's a good lie all right, but after two or three nights, she gets boring. Have you tried Emenzabel?"

"Not yet but she looks all right. I'll give her a go when the opportunity comes up," replied Adonijah.

You both totally disgust me," said Absalom.

With that, Absalom withdrew from the company of his brothers and left them boasting to one another about what they would do when they had harems of their own. I won't report their conversation lest you, the reader, should think I am straying into the realms of pornography.

It's clear from the conversation just recorded that Amnon had a penchant for Absalom's sister, Tamar, but she had wisely made a point of avoiding him. Amnon sought advice from Jonadab, one of his cousins who had noticed how dejected Amnon was looking. Amnon described his unrequited love for Tamar (Amnon's word 'love' isn't really the correct word to convey the lust concealed in his mind.) Jonadab was shrewd and well meaning. He could be counted upon to come up with good ideas. Without realising what Amnon might have had in mind, Jonadab suggested that Amnon should feign sickness and ask his father to send Tamar round to his house with some food. This would provide the opportunity for him to get to know her.

Amnon followed this advice. In due course, an unsuspecting Tamar arrived at Amnon's house, bearing some bread she had baked. She was shown into Amnon's room where he was lying in bed, apparently unwell. Amnon sent everyone else out of the room and in spite of Tamar's protests, he raped her.

It's strange what conscience can do to a person's mind. Having raped his half-sister, Amnon's love (lust?) for her suddenly turned to intense hatred. He had his servants turn Tamar out and bolt the door behind her.[50]

Tamar was devastated. She had dressed in her best clothes for this visit to Amnon She tore these clothes into rags and returned home weeping. Absalom took her in and did his best to comfort her. Tamar was feeling absolutely desolate. Absalom promised Tamar that this deed would be avenged. From that time, he never spoke to Amnon but nursed a deep hatred in his heart, waiting the right moment to execute his vengeance. King David was furious when he heard what had happened. After all, he was the one who had sent Tamar on this errand to Amnon's house. In spite of his fury, David remained the inadequate parent, taking no corrective action against his wayward son.

Absalom waited two years to enact his revenge. One day, he held a party to celebrate a successful harvest of wool from his flocks and invited David and the whole of the royal household to come to the event. As Absalom had expected, David declined the invitation but as Absalom was insistent, David sent Amnon, his eldest son, as his representative. Did the king naively think that this was an act of reconciliation between the brothers who had been at daggers drawn since the time of Tamar's rape?

Absalom knew his brother well and how given he was to excess. Absalom ordered his men to kill Amnon, once he had drunk to such an extent that he'd become obnoxious and incapable. Absalom surely knew he would degenerate into such a state. Absalom's men were initially wary about carrying out this order but Absalom reassured them that there would be no repercussions. They were acting under his authority.

Thus it was, when the party was in full swing with most of David's family there, having a good time, Amnon got well and truly drunk and started to behave in a disgusting and provocative way. Absalom's men responded to this and his senior servant struck Amnon down and killed him with a single dagger thrust to the throat. Panic stricken, the king's sons all dashed out in confusion. It took a little while for them to find their horses and make for home. Meanwhile, a messenger reached David ahead of his sons with the misinformation that Absalom had killed all the King's sons. At that news, the King and those with him rent their clothes, a characteristic action in those times in response to receiving devastating news. The King prostrated himself on the ground and the others stood by in shock horror.

Jonadab realised that Absalom's sole argument was with his brother, Amnon, and that he wouldn't have harmed the others. He had feared that Absalom might contemplate doing something like this from the time Amnon had raped Tamar. Jonadab reassured David that the only one of his sons likely to have been killed was Amnon. The rest would return home safely. Sure enough, the sentry keeping watch at the city gate reported that a large crowd was coming down the hill at great speed towards the city.

"These are your sons returning safely as I told you they would," said Jonadab to the King and sure enough, they arrived at the palace in a state of some distress to report to David what had happened.[51]

In the meantime, Absalom fled and took refuge with Talmad, King of Geshur.

David mourned the death of Amnon. However, he seemed to be far more concerned that Absalom, who was largely regarded to be David's favourite son, had now departed from the kingdom in the most unpleasant of circumstances..

One might have hoped this his brother's untimely death would have had a salutary effect on Adonijah, but no, he continued to be his loud, obnoxious self. This is evidenced by the lewd way he accosted Abishag on one of her visits to the palace to visit her friends in David's harem. The fact that Abishag was known to be betrothed to Benaiah, who was now a senior officer in the army, didn't cause Adonijah to moderate his tone or the way he addressed Abishag.

"You look a bit of 'all right' today Abishag, but then, you always do. I don't suppose Benaiah kicks you out of bed but if he does, feel welcome to come and share mine!"

This remark was doubly insulting for it implied that he didn't believe that Benaiah and Abishag would be waiting until they were properly married before consummating their marriage. Abishag felt debased by Adonijah's comment. Benaiah was appalled that Abishag should have been subject to such a crude remark by the king's son but for the time being there was little he could do to curb Adonijah's unruly tongue.

Chapter 9

Gilgal and Machpelah

The nation of Israel was now entering a phase of relative stability. They were easily the dominant nationality in the land and the need for wars with the neighbouring tribes, necessary for self-preservation, was no longer there. Benaiah and his friend Zalmon were able to take leave from their military duties but had no clear idea about what to do with this time of relaxation. Zalmon had a very beautiful girlfriend, Atarah, an Ephraimite and therefore, from the same tribe as Benaiah and Zalmon. Benaiah and Abishag, Zalmon and Atarah, formed a foursome of very close friends who enjoyed doing things together. The four of them met together to discuss what they might do during this time of leave.

Abishag came up with a suggestion.

"I would like to visit the monuments which mark our nation's antiquity. I know that great buildings exist in Nineveh and Babylon. I've heard of the pyramids in Egypt. Some claim that they were built by our people when they were Pharaoh's slaves but I understand that the Egyptians refute this. They say that the pyramids were built by themselves and not as slaves but as a paid workforce. In any case, the pyramids are not in Israel. What do we have as a durable mark of our own nation in Israel?"

None of them had an answer to this but they knew someone who would know, - Zadok the priest. They arranged to meet with him. Zadok welcomed this opportunity to get to know these young people better and indeed, to provide them with information concerning Israel's history. He agreed that, as yet, Israel was very limited in monuments which would speak of their past to future generations of Israelite people. Israel was, at this point in time, a very young nation whose history in the land of Israel itself, only extended back a relatively small number of years. However, he assured them that as time moved on, buildings which spoke of Israel's proud history would be built. Zadok then directed them to a site in Israel which had particular historical significance to the people of Israel.

"When Joshua crossed the River Jordan, and the Israelites first set foot in this land, he commanded them to build a cairn of twelve stones, one for each of the tribes of Israel, with stones excavated from the bed of the Jordan. At the time, this was possible because God had created a dry path across the Jordan to enable the Israelites to enter the land he had promised to give them. However, they would have to work quickly because the Jordan would soon flow back to follow its normal course and the bed of the river would no longer be accessible. This cairn is still there, indeed, I believe that it is even larger now than that created with the original twelve stones because pilgrims have added their own stones to the cairn as they visit the site." [52]

Atarah had a question for Zadok.
"Why only twelve stones and not thirteen? There are thirteen tribes of Israel descended from Jacob."

Zadok had an answer.
"When the Israelites were still in Egypt and Jacob had become very old, the time came for him to bestow blessings on his sons. He had twelve sons and it was traditional for the eldest son to receive a double blessing but Jacob departed from tradition. His eldest sons had greatly disappointed him and so he bestowed the special blessing on Joseph. It wasn't just that Joseph was his favourite son. Joseph had been the agent by which the rest of the family had been saved from starvation. So therefore, Joseph had the double blessing and his two sons became the heads of two extra tribes, your tribe of Ephraim and the tribe of Manasseh. Here again, Jacob departed from tradition and crossed over his hands so that his right hand rested on the head of the youngest of Joseph's sons, Ephraim. This signified

that he was the one who would receive the greater blessing. Ephraim and Manasseh, together with Jacob's other eleven sons are the patriarchs of Israel's thirteen tribes."[53]

As the young folk listened, Zadok continued,

"Because they had so displeased him, Jacob effectively disinherited two of his older sons, Simeon and Levi,[54] and no land was to be reserved for them when the nation of Israel entered the promised land where we live now.[55] The tribe of Levi, the tribe into which Moses and Aaron were born, does not have an identifiable territory in Israel but has taken on the priestly function of the nation. This means that members of the tribe of Levi, that is my tribe, are dispersed among all the other tribes to serve as priests. Simeon is one of the smallest, if not the smallest, tribe of Israel, but the descendants of Simeon do exist as a de facto tribe even though they come outside the scope of Jacob's blessing. Nonetheless, they have been allocated land to the south of the territory occupied by the tribe of Judah. Thus, the tribe of Simeon barely has a separate identity and is being absorbed into Judah. So then, if you discount Simeon as a tribe in its own right, you revert to the special number of twelve tribes."

The four young people listened intrigued with Zadok's exposition as they learnt something of the origin of the tribal identities about which they had previously been ignorant.

Abishag then asked,
"Historically, the entry of Joshua into the land occupied by the Canaanites is a relatively recent event. Is there no monument or building in this land which would take us back to an earlier time in our nation's history?"

Zadok replied,
"Indeed there is. There's a shrine which goes back to our patriarch, Abraham, no less. When Abraham's wife, Sarah died, he bought a burial site at a place called Machpelah near Hebron from Ephron who was a Hittite.[56] Sarah was buried there and in due course, Abraham[57] was too. Isaac and Rebecca are buried there. So too are Jacob and Leah.[58] Indeed, the body of Jacob was carried there, all the way from Egypt, so that he could lie at rest with his forefathers. I haven't been there but I understand that this burial site is well guarded and cared for."

This information resonated in Benaiah's mind with what Uriah had told him about his ancestor selling a burial site to Abraham.

Atarah reflected, "That must indeed be the earliest monument with connections to our nation in this land, unless you, Zadok, are aware of anything more ancient. Is there anything as old as the pyramids?"

"Not in the land of Israel, but near Abraham's birthplace at Ur[59] in Babylon, there is a great tower which is known as a ziggurat. Some say that this was the Tower of Babel which our foolish forefathers built because they thought that by so doing, they would be able to reach heaven and God himself!"[60]

"I don't think we'll have time to travel that far," said Zalmon, "but thank you for telling us about the cairn at Gilgal and the burial site at Machpelah. These will be wonderful objectives to discover during this time of leave from military duties."

The four young people returned to their homes in a state of excited expectancy. This holiday would not be just a few days of aimless leisure but they would have sites of great significance to visit. The following day, they set off on four, strong, military horses and took with them the minimum of gear they would need to set up camp. Benaiah had studied the maps held at the military headquarters and he knew the way they should proceed to get first to Gilgal. Benaiah and Zalmon carried swords which they hoped would not be needed but they were confident that they were strong and able enough to ward off an enemy if attacked on their journey. It so happened that their journey wasn't without incident.

After a few hours, they encountered a small party who seemed to be in some distress and had stopped by the side of the route on which they were travelling. From their dress, they could be recognised as Amalekites. Our foursome stopped and the leader of this group of Amalekites explained that his sister had gone prematurely into labour and there was no one in the group who knew anything about delivering a baby. Abishag had helped out at the maternity wing of David's harem which she frequently visited and volunteered her services. Atarah was a very hands-on type of person and between them, they safely delivered the baby. The Amalekites were overcome with gratitude and invited them to share a meal before continuing on their way. An interesting discussion ensued.

"How is it that you Israelites have been prepared to help us Amalekites?" their leader asked. "We always thought that hostility existed between our people and realise that much of the fault lies with ourselves. We know that our people attacked your forefathers in Sinai as they journeyed to this land[61] and not so long ago, a raiding party from our people attacked Ziklag and carried off your cattle and womenfolk.[62] Sufficient to say, I didn't approve of this and had nothing to do with that attack but I would fully expect to be identified as a member of the tribe who carried out this deed."

Benaiah and Zalmon had almost fond memories of this action as it was their first involvement in warfare.

"All our women and livestock were recovered intact" replied Benaiah. "They had been well treated. Actions like the one you describe are the responsibility of the leaders of a nation. Its people have no alternative but to comply with their leader's orders. As a soldier, I've been bound by this discipline and I've even seen my own nation, of which I'm usually justifiably proud, carry out actions of which I am ashamed. We don't judge anyone on the basis of their race or tribe. Each individual deserves to be considered as a unique individual with their own strengths and weaknesses."

The Amalekites listened thoughtfully to Benaiah's words.

"We are aware that good and bad people exist among all people and nations including our own and we reserve judgement on individuals until we have come to know them really well. Ordinary people are much the same the world over and are not inclined to make war on their neighbours. We bear no grudge against anyone because of the folly of their leadership. No, we are glad to be able to help fellow humans who find themselves in a distressing situation, regardless of race or tribe."

Benaiah then explained how faith in his God influenced his attitudes towards others.

"As Israelites, we are pleased to welcome any into our nation, any who are prepared to see the folly of worshipping impotent idols made of wood or stone and recognise that there is but one true God. This God we call Jehovah, revealed himself to our ancestors and continues to care for and protect his people. He is spirit and cannot be seen but he is everywhere around us and we are conscious of his working in our midst."

Benaiah went on to explain how others who were not born as Israelites had come to accept Jehovah as their God.

"I am an army commander of two regiments who are not Israelite by birth[63] but whose members have come to acknowledge the supremacy of Jehovah. Our king, David, has an army commander from the Philistine city of Gath[64], leading a loyal regiment of soldiers recruited from the same city. They were formerly our enemies but now, they too have recognised the supremacy of Jehovah and have sworn allegiance to him."

Benaiah realised that he would have to explain why the Israelites appeared to be so belligerent towards other tribes.

"The reason that we are so often found fighting tribes like your own and we avoid marrying outside our nation is because of a fear that idol worship could enter into our nation like an infectious disease. When Jehovah founded our nation, it was not to fight others. On the contrary, Jehovah declared that our nation was there to bring a blessing to all people.[65] Sadly, not all our people have taken this concept on board but we're not 'all our people'. If we've done something today which you regard as a blessing, then we're satisfied that we've pleased Jehovah. You Amalekites, like ourselves, are descendants of Abraham and Isaac."

Benaiah's long speech was followed by a silence during which it could be clearly seen that the Amalekites were carefully considering what Benaiah had said.

The silence was broken by the leader of the Amalekites who reiterated his thanks for what they had done in safely delivering his sister's child and he added thanks for the words that Benaiah had just spoken. He described them as 'words of great wisdom'.

The Amalekites broke camp to continue on their way with their new-born baby. Now that the emergency which had caused them to stop had been dealt with, our foursome continued on their way to Jericho. They knew that Gilgal couldn't be far from this city and they reached Jericho as dusk was gathering. The scattered buildings which represented what had once been a proud city were no longer protected by a city wall. Joshua had pronounced a curse on any who rebuilt Jericho's walls[66] but Hiel the Bethelite braved this curse many years later and rebuilt the walls during the reign of Ahab at the expense of his eldest and youngest sons.[67] It was too dark now to go sight-seeing so they entered Jericho and found a comfortable hostelry where they could stable the horses and stay and be fed. They were comfortably tired and were glad not to have to put up their tents in the fading light after their long journey.

The following day, their innkeeper directed them to the cairn at Gilgal. As Zadok had predicted, the cairn had grown considerably from the twelve original stones laid after Joshua and the Israelites had miraculously crossed the Jordan, dry shod. The friends added stones of their own to this monument which marked the point at which the Israelites entered into the promised land. After spending many awestruck minutes surveying this monument of great significance to their nation, they set off for Machpelah, several miles to the north. On their way they experienced another encounter which was so very different from their meeting with the Amalekites the previous day.

Coming towards them was a small caravan of camels bearing goods intended to be traded, possibly in Egypt. Half a dozen young men from the caravan stepped out and appeared to be intent on barring the way.

"Who are you and where are you going?" they demanded.

"We are citizens of Jerusalem and where we are bound is no concern of yours," responded Benaiah.

One of the young men spat on the ground and retorted,

"A curse be on the tribe of Judah. The kingdom rightly belongs to the descendants of Saul and not to this jumped up David shepherd boy."

The plaid on his clothing marked him out as a Benjaminite.

"We are not Judeans but Ephraimites, descendants of Jacob's wife, Rachel, as are the Benjaminites,"[68] responded Benaiah. "For the sake of our nation, you would do well to bury this rancour against David and his tribe. Jerusalem is full of members of every tribe of Israel[130] as well as others who have renounced their idols in deference to Jehovah. If we are to survive in this land, we must put aside tribal rivalries and unite as a single people. The northern tribes have already accepted David as their rightful king. What makes you so different?"

Benaiah and Zalmon wheeled their horses and the Benjaminites could see they carried swords and looked as if they knew how to use them.

"Be on your way then," said another in the group and they returned to their caravan which had halted while those remaining with the caravan had focused inquisitive eyes on the encounter which was taking place.

The caravan moved off and the friends continued on their way to Machpelah. To start with, they rode in silence, thinking of the implications for the nation of Israel if many members of the northern tribes harboured this resentment against David. However, they soon began to chatter cheerfully among themselves again. They tended to ride in pairs as this made conversation easier for people travelling on horseback. Sometimes, the two men rode together, just ahead of Abishag and Atarah who chatted away in the rear. More often than not though, Benaiah rode with Abishag and Zalmon with Atarah. They now had opportunities for deep, personal conversations which were difficult to fit in amid the business of work and the hectic life they led in Jerusalem.

"I was so impressed with the way you helped the Amalekite family and safely delivered their baby," said Benaiah. "You're not just a very beautiful woman but a very practical one too."

"That's been one of the advantages of helping out at the harem when I go to visit my friends," replied Abishag. "It's surprising the range of skills you pick up when you're always ready to lend a hand there. It was a great help to have Atarah to assist me when we stopped to help those Amalekites. I was so proud of the way that you and Zalmon stood up to that gang of Benjaminites. I was afraid there was going to be a fight but, although we were outnumbered, I really felt secure and protected with the two of you there."

"I don't think we were in much danger," responded Benaiah. "Zalmon and I are experienced soldiers and I don't suppose any of those Benjaminites had ever been involved in a real battle. But that brings me to another problem. I love you so much, Abishag, and I'm so looking forward to the time we may marry in security and bring up a family. Do you regret the pact we made that we should not marry until I was out of the army?"

"I would marry you tomorrow and hope that I could cope with the grief I would feel should I lose you. Indeed, that would be a difficult thing to bear even as a betrothed bride as I am now. When you're away, I'm in a state of continuous anxiety which gives place to rapturous joy when you return. The thing I would find difficult is having to tell my children that their father wasn't coming home should I lose you at a time when we had a family. I've witnessed how bereft women and their children are when the army returns without their husband and father who's been lost in battle. Why do we have to live in a world where there is so much fighting?"

They rode on in silence for a while as they considered the implications of their conversation. Benaiah broke the silence.

"What a wonderful woman you are to deny yourself in a really big matter out of consideration of how the things you do and the decisions you make will affect others. Are you really happy, Abishag?"

Abishag didn't have to pause to give a well-considered thoughtful reply. She knew that she was happy.

"I am deliriously happy, Benaiah. I'm the envy of all my friends to be betrothed to the great Benaiah. You not only have the reputation of being one of the greatest warriors in the army, but at the same time, you're so considerate and gentle when at home and away from the demands imposed by military campaigns."

It was well on into the afternoon when they finally reached Machpelah. They decided to wait until the following morning before going sightseeing. They pitched their tents and went into nearby Hebron to buy food and drink before returning to get an early night.

The following day dawned bright and after a light breakfast, the foursome made their way to the sacred mausoleum. As Zadok had said, it was very clean and well cared for. Two guards stood at the entrance where they exchanged pleasantries before being ushered into the building. There were several well-tended graves but beautifully embroidered draperies adorned the special shrines. These were the resting places of Abraham and Sarah; Isaac and Rebecca; and Jacob and Leah.[58] The guard who had explained what was there to be seen, left them to remain in awesome silence as they contemplated the last resting places of these revered patriarchs and matriarchs. These were the ones who had founded their proud nation, and more than that, who had instilled a sense of the importance of living in close relationship with the all-powerful and omniscient God in whose hands rested the eternity of every living person.

They spent an hour in this shrine, enjoying the ambience, immersed in peace and relishing the silence, for they passed this time alone. Their delight in this experience was not interrupted by other visitors entering the sanctuary.

They left the shrine, thanked the guards and then proceeded homewards. They chatted less as they allowed the recollection of their recent experience to infuse their minds.

On receiving news of their return to Jerusalem, Zadok arranged to meet with them to learn of their experiences. This time, he had arranged for Nathan to be with him. They described all that had happened, not so much with enthusiasm but with peaceful pleasure. Zadok and Nathan were pleased with the way they had helped the Amalekites but disturbed by the account of their confrontation with the Benjaminites.

"The Israelites are setting too much store by their physical hereditary," pronounced Nathan, "and too little to spirituality. The restriction on intermarriage with gentiles was imposed, not because the gentiles are inferior to us as people but because of the danger of being absorbed into the culture of idolatry practised by the gentile tribes among whom we live. Many of the proselytes who have become absorbed into our nation and faith have a far greater appreciation of the spiritual importance of being an Israelite than many who claim to be directly descended from Abraham. You will know that, Benaiah, from your regiments of Kerethites and Pelethites. Even David himself had a Moabite grandmother called Ruth and a Canaanite great-grandmother called Rahab.[69] Moses wife, Zipporah, was a Midianite. Your ancestor, Joseph, was married to an Egyptian called Asenath. However, it didn't take intermarriage with idolaters and polytheists for the Israelites to turn to idols. No sooner was Moses back turned during the wilderness journey than they made themselves a golden calf to worship. If the nation persists in this notion of racial superiority because they regard themselves as God's special people, they're in for a rude awakening. They'll be conquered by other nations and deported. Sadly, they won't learn from their mistakes. When they return to their own land, they'll continue to treat others as inferior. God declared that Abraham's descendants were to bring great blessing to all people[65] but regretably, that blessing will come largely through one descendant, the Messiah, and the few Israelites who respond to his call. You showed yourself to be true Israelites in the pattern God requires of his people when you helped those unfortunate Amalekites."

The four young people left that meeting, the thoughts that the prophet Nathan had shared being added to their special recollections of the few days they had spent together, visiting two important antiquities of the nation.

Chapter 10

Thoughts on the future of Israel

Senior members among those who held important positions in the kingdom began to give serious thought as to who should succeed David as king, for David was showing signs of aging. Now that Amnon was dead and Absalom banished, Adonijah was the eldest surviving son and no-one saw him as a person suitable to inherit the throne. Many discussions on this issue were held by little groups meeting in secret.

Joab, the general of the army, and Ahithophel, one of the wise men on David's council, had formed a good relationship with Absalom and felt their futures would be most secure if he was the new king. However, unless Absalom could be reconciled with David and return in safety to Jerusalem, there was no chance that would happen.

Meanwhile, Nathan, Zadok, Hushai and Benaiah had become aware that another possibility was arising. Bathsheba's son, Jedidiah[47], commonly known as Solomon, was growing from boyhood to youth and displaying remarkable intelligence.

"This young man shows considerable potential," remarked Hushai. "I could even describe him as a prodigy."

"I've noticed that too," added Benaiah, "but unless some care is taken in his upbringing, especially during these formative years, he'll end up just like the rest of David's sons, good for nothing!"

Nathan endorsed Benaiah's assessment.

"You're right, Benaiah. The lad needs a good education and discipline, and he specially needs good male role models. I don't think that I'm being unduly boastful or arrogant if I suggest that between us, we could provide those elements in Solomon's upbringing that have been so sorely lacking in the way the rest of David's sons have been brought up."

"Nathan and I could see to the religious side of the boy's education," volunteered Zadok. "I could give him a good grounding in the law delivered to Moses and Nathan could see to it that he has a good understanding of the history of our people, both good and bad. We can't pretend that our own nation hasn't often gone astray and a king of Israel needs to be aware of the pitfalls to avoid as well as the glorious aspects of our history."

Nathan identified the remaining aspects of Solomon's education which would need to be provided, identifying members of the group who might cover these areas in which instruction would be required.

"You'd be the ideal person to teach Solomon numeracy and literacy, how to write good Hebrew and coherently present arguments," he said to Hushai "and you, Benaiah, can train the boy in the art of warfare, not just how to use weapons but how to marshal and organise an army and the tactics suitable for modern warfare. Most importantly, you will need to explain how the army is provided with all the food and drink its needs when on campaign."

They all nodded in agreement to these suggestions.

"However," said Hushai, "we won't be able to put these ideas into practice without the agreement of the boy's mother."

"I can arrange that," said Nathan. "I've spent a lot of time counselling her, especially after that shameful affair when she committed adultery with David. She lost not only the true husband she loved but her new-born son to the bargain. Very little of the blame for that disgraceful episode can be laid at Bathsheba's door. The power of an absolute monarch like David is such that he commands and you have no alternative but to obey. Bathsheba is a wise and intelligent woman. That's probably the source of much of Solomon's wisdom. From things I've already said to her, I know that she'll be in full agreement with what we've just discussed. She now needs to subtlety work on David to ensure that he identifies Solomon as his successor when the time comes."

Joab used rather different tactics to bring about the possibility of his favoured candidate succeeding David. On several occasions, he'd asked David to forgive and restore his son, Absalom, to favour but to no avail. Joab therefore adopted a more cunning approach to get David to change his mind. He took a leaf from Nathan's book, knowing the way Nathan had approached David to confront him with the murder of Uriah.

Joab knew of a woman in Tekoa who had built up a reputation for tact and diplomacy in dealing with interpersonal problems which had been brought to her. Joab explained his objective to her and asked this woman to dress herself in mourning clothes and approach David as a distressed widow at the time that David regularly set aside to hear petitions from his people. The story Joab had concocted for the woman to bring to David was that one of her two sons had killed the other when they got into a fight during an argument.

She was to say that the son who had won the fight had gone away into hiding. When she discovered the reason for the dispute, the widow was to tell David that she realised that her surviving son had good reason to fight with his brother. The woman's neighbours had disagreed with her assessment and were insistent that this son should be executed for committing murder. This would leave her destitute, so she was to ask David for his advice..

The woman of Tekoa carried out Joab's instructions perfectly.

The king said to her, "Go home and tell your son it's safe to return. I will issue a decree that no-one should harm him."

Then, in a rather roundabout way, the woman indicated that the king himself had left his own son in exile. Why had he done this when he could so easily have issued a decree giving his son safe conduct to return home? Had she used words like those Nathan had used when he had confronted the king over a situation where David was at fault, the widow would have made her point by saying to the king,
"You are the man who has caused his son to have to remain in exile."

David was astute enough to recognise that Joab was behind the request this woman had made, as Joab himself had pleaded unsuccessfully for the restoration of Absalom on several occasions. David challenged the woman to admit that she had come to him with this petition in response to a request from Joab. The woman complimented David on his astuteness and admitted that this was indeed the case.[72]

David sent for Joab and gave him leave to go to Geshur with the news that the king had given Absalom safe conduct to return to Jerusalem. Joab prostrated himself before the king in gratitude for his clemency and travelled to Geshur to bear these tidings to Absalom.[73]

Absalom returned to Jerusalem, much to the dismay of the party who wished to see Solomon succeed David. However, things didn't initially work out quite as Absalom had hoped. Absalom lived for two years in Jerusalem but the king refused to see him. Absalom sent several messages to Joab, asking him to arrange a meeting with David, but Joab ignored his requests.[74]

Absalom began to get impatient. Not being a person who was afraid of taking drastic action to realize his purpose, Absalom arranged for one of his servants to burn the field of barley belonging to Joab which was adjacent to his own field. This did bring Joab running, challenging Absalom to explain why his servants had set his barley crop alight. Absalom explained that he had to do this to get Joab to listen to his requests because Joab was just ignoring the polite messages Absalom had been sending him.

"I am more than ready to meet my father," said Absalom. "If he can show good reason why I should be put to death, then I am prepared to face execution."

So it was, Joab arranged this meeting between Absalom and his father. Absalom respectfully bowed low before his father. David couldn't resist showing his affection for the one he regarded as a special son and hugged and kissed the much-loved son who had been so long out of his presence.[75]

With Amnon dead, Absalom was now the eldest son. In no time, he started to behave like a king in waiting. He acquired a magnificent chariot and would ride round the city, accompanied by his bodyguard of fifty carefully chosen men. He would frequently sit at the city gate and invite any coming into the city with a petition to present to the king to let him see this petition. Having scanned the petition, he would invariably say that this is a just petition and should receive a favourable answer from the king. However, he would explain, that the king is only allotting a small amount of time to receiving petitions and this petition is unlikely to be heard. Absalom would then add in a voice that could easily be overheard,

"How I wish that I was at least a judge in Israel (using the title ascribed to the former rulers of Israel). I would ensure that important representations like your own would be heard and acted upon."

Absalom would enquire about which city the petitioner had come from in the hope that on his return home, the petitioner would take back a good report of Absalom, so earning him a good reputation in parts of the country which he might need to rely on for support in the future.

As Absalom walked around town, any who greeted him by bowing in obeisance, would receive a hug and kiss to their hand. In such ways, Absalom gained the respect and affection of the people.[76]

Nathan, Zadok, Hushai and Benaiah met to take stock of the situation.

"As David's eldest and favourite son and a prince who's growing in popularity with the people," began Nathan, "it's highly likely that Absalom will be nominated by David as his successor and become the next king,"

"Where does this leave our favoured candidate?" asked Benaiah. "Solomon is still in his mid-teens."

Zadok and Hushai expressed their concern that with the return and growing popularity of Absalom, Solomon was unlikely to become prime candidate to inherit the crown. They were somewhat dismayed about this and described how well Solomon was shaping up under their instruction. He really had the makings of a someone who would be a great king.

Nathan told them that his prophetic instinct still told him that Solomon would indeed be the next king but that it was important to defer to God's will in this matter. He suggested that they should pray about this, as indeed, they had done frequently since Absalom first went into exile.

"We must pray for both Absalom and Solomon, and of course, for David. We mustn't be too specific, praying that our candidate, Solomon, should be king but rather, that the next king should be someone of God's choice. Who knows? Absalom may indeed become a great king when the time comes."

So they prayed along these lines.

Chapter 11

Absalom's rebellion

Patience is a virtue. Impatience is a vice. Absalom was not a patient person. Here he was, a king in waiting and his father whom he felt was past it, was still clinging to power. Absalom had been hanging around in Jerusalem for the past four years. He was popular with the people and yet powerless to exert any real influence on the way the country was run. To change the status quo, he'd need to effect a coup d'etat. How could this be accomplished? A plan began to formulate itself in Absalom's mind.

Absalom went to David with a request.

"During the years I was in exile in Geshur, I yearned for a time when I would be able to return to Jerusalem. I prayed to God and vowed that if ever I should be fortunate enough to come back to this city, I would express my thanks to him by offering a sacrifice. The years have passed and I haven't fulfilled my vow. Permit me therefore, to go to Hebron, your former capital city, to make this sacrifice."

"By all means, Absalom," David replied. "Go with my blessing."

Absalom departed for Hebron, taking with him a small army. He sent for Ahithophel, one of David's senior advisers and councillors, to join him in Hebron. He secretly sent messengers to key cities in Israel to say that the trumpet call which would be sounded from town to town in Israel, would be to signify that Absalom was proclaimed the new King of Israel.[77]

When the news of what Absalom was doing reached David, he was overcome with shock and dismay. During these years of relative peace and quiet, David had not maintained a strong army in Jerusalem. He was defended by the Kerethites and Pelethites, his personal bodyguard under the command of Benaiah, and a regiment of mercenaries under Ittai, the Gittite. This was an inadequate force to defeat the much larger army that would return to Jerusalem under Absalom. David knew that Absalom had become very popular with the people of Jerusalem and he therefore knew that he couldn't rely on their support when Absalom returned to the city. David was left with the stark realisation that he had no alternative but to flee the city with his personal bodyguard until he could build up the strength of his own support. As Ittai was a mercenary, David urged him to return to his own country but Ittai was utterly loyal. He refused to withdraw his support from

David, even if it meant risking his own life by not taking an easy way out of the danger now threatening.[78]

So it was, David left Jerusalem accompanied by his personal bodyguard under Benaiah and the men serving under Ittai. He left the palace to be looked after by his concubines under their mistress, Eglah. Zadok and Abiathar, the priests, followed David a short time later, meeting up with him at his camp in the desert region on the other side of the river Jordan. They brought the Ark of the Covenant with them. This was received with great acclaim by those with David who regarded this as a sign that God was with them.

David took counsel with Zadok and Abiathar.

"I will need people in Jerusalem whom I can trust and who can keep me informed of what's happening," explained David. "I therefore think it best if both of you, along with your sons, Ahimaaz and Jonathan, return with the Ark to Jerusalem, posing as Israelites who were prepared to give their loyalty to Absalom. Your sons can bring me news of any developments in Jerusalem which I'll need to know about as soon as they take place."[79]

David had heard that one of his two main counsellors, Ahithophel, had joined Absalom. His other senior counsellor, Hushai, joined David at his camp in the desert region. Ahithophel's defection had been of serious concern to David because Ahithophel was an intelligent man and could offer Absalom sound advice on how to defeat David and consolidate his hold on the throne. Hushai was the only other person who might be able to offer alternative advice which would counter anything suggested by Ahithophel. Knowing that Hushai was utterly loyal to himself, David asked Hushai to join Absalom to become part of his advisory team and thwart any guidance coming from Ahithophel.

David explained his thinking to Hushai,

"If Absalom follows the advice of Ahithophel which will surely be to hunt us down as soon as possible before we've had time to gather forces and build up our own strength, we're certainly doomed. However, if you can counter Ahithophel's advice and suggest to Absalom that he should delay launching any attack on ourselves, this'll give us the time we need to consolidate our forces and build up an army which will be strong enough to defeat Absalom."[80]

This then was David's objective as he continued on his journey away from Jerusalem. On the way, he encountered a diversion which could have led to a skirmish as he passed through territory belonging to a Benjaminite named Shimei. David avoided the temptation to respond to the provocation he was receiving. Had David responded, he would have doubtlessly won the encounter but it would have been at the expense of losing men during the engagement. With such a small force under his command at this time, incurring casualties was something David could ill afford. A more serious conflict with the forces of Absalom was likely to take place soon. David would then need all the manpower he could muster.

The diversion came as David and his men approached Bahurim. Shimei, a close relative of Saul, appeared with a gang of his men at the top of a ridge which defined one side of the valley through which David was passing. He started to pelt David's party with stones and yelled abuse at him.

"This serves you right for all the damage you did to Saul and his family," he shouted. "God's given the kingdom over to your son, Absalom, because you're just a bloodthirsty tyrant!"

Benaiah and his men were raring to mount the ridge and give Shimei and his gang the lesson they deserved but they were restrained by David who was in a very depressed mood.

"Let them be," commanded David. "A few sticks and stones thrown at us aren't going to do us any real harm. Neither will Shimei's angry words. If my own son with no cause can turn against me, so much more will relatives of Saul, for they may well consider that they have a genuine grievance against me. I will leave the judgement to God. Either God has told Shimei to behave in the way he just has or, if not, he will turn Shimei's curses into blessings."[81]

David and his small entourage continued on their way, leaving the territory controlled by Shimei until they reached a suitable site to pitch camp. They were all totally exhausted by having to march at some speed to get away from Jerusalem quickly and were glad to settle for the night and recuperate.

Meanwhile, Absalom was consolidating his own hold on Jerusalem, relying strongly on any advice given by Ahithophel.

Ahithophel said to Absalom, "It's the usual practice when one king takes over from another that he also takes over the former king's harem to show everyone that now, he's fully in control. I therefore suggest that you do just that but make sure that everyone in Jerusalem is fully aware that you have done this.

Instead of remaining within the privacy of the palace, erect a tent on the roof of the palace to accommodate the harem. In this way, everyone in Jerusalem will be able to see you when you enter the tent to take over the harem." [82]

Absalom followed this advice.

This fulfilled a prophecy which Nathan had made when he reprimanded David over his affair with Bathsheba.[83]

2 Samuel ch 12 v 11,12   *This is what the Lord says :- "Out of your own household I am going to bring calamity upon you. Before your very eyes, I will take your wives and give them to one who is close to you, and he will lie with your wives in broad daylight. You did it in secret, but I will do this thing in broad daylight before all Israel."*

Among those who came to congratulate Absalom on becoming king was David's friend, Hushai, who was renowned for the wisdom in the advice he proffered, no less than Ahithophel.

"Long live the king! Long live the king!" proclaimed Hushai as he came into Absalom's presence.

Absalom regarded Hushai with suspicion.

"How is it that such a great friend of David's should abandon him to join my cause?" he asked.

"It's clear that you are now the rightful king of Israel," Hushai replied. "Look how you are acclaimed by the people of this city while David has retreated like a defeated cur after a dog fight. I make service to the rightful king as my priority in life. As I served David when he was king, so now, I offer my services to you."[84]

In view of his reputation for great wisdom and his ability to give sound advice, Hushai was admitted into the circle of Absalom's wise men and advisers. Absalom convened a council of his chief men and advisers and sought first, any advice that Ahithophel might give.

"I would strike now, while David is weak and disorganised. He left Jerusalem with no more than a thousand men. Don't delay. Select twelve thousand men and start your pursuit tonight. When you reach David's force, concentrate your attack on David and try to reduce casualties among the rest of his following. Once David is dead, they'll have nothing left to fight for. Although at first, they'll flee, they'll soon realise that they've been beaten and David is no longer there.

Then they'll have no alternative but to return and offer you their allegiance. You'll be the only king whom they can serve."[85]

Meanwhile, Hushai was thinking on his feet. He realised that if Ahithophel's advice prevailed, David would be lost. With the few men with him now, he couldn't possibly hold out against an army of twelve thousand men. However, the men with Absalom now weren't seasoned soldiers, experienced in battle, but like Absalom, they were just thirsty for glory. Hushai knew that David needed him to give advice which would buy him the time needed to build up his force and regroup. Hushai thought of just the advice to proffer to buy David this much needed time.

Absalom called on Hushai next to share his thoughts on the situation. Hushai was diplomatic in the way he presented his case.

"Much of Ahithophel's advice is excellent. When the time comes to attack David, killing David should be the attacking force's sole objective. As Ahithophel advised, it's important to limit the casualties inflicted on the rest of David's force. This then will result in your more speedily receiving support of those who were on David's side, for as Ahithophel says, they'll have no other king to whom to owe allegiance."

Having started by endorsing Ahithophel's advice, Hushai continued on a different track.

"However, I don't agree with the rest of Ahithophel's advice. David may have left Jerusalem with only a thousand men at arms but he'll pick up support on the way to his new headquarters. David's men are largely battle hardened, experienced soldiers who have fought in campaigns against such redoubtable foes as the Ammonites, the Moabites, the Amalekites and, let us not forget, the Philistines. David's men have highly experienced commanders too, men like Joab, Abishai, Ittai and Benaiah. They've fought and defeated much larger armies than their own, very much against the odds but prevailing because they had the experience and valour to do so."

Hushai then challenged Ahithophel's estimate of the relative numerical strength of the two sides.

"Ahithophel suggested that you should pursue David tonight with twelve thousand men. This just might be good enough odds to defeat David's force of one thousand men, but since he left Jerusalem, David will have been adding daily to his number, and his strength may be now two thousand, perhaps even three thousand men at arms."

Hushai looked Absalom in the eye.

"Will you, Absalom, be able to raise a force of twelve thousand experienced soldiers by the evening to set off in pursuit? I think not. At best, by this evening, you may have been able to summon eight thousand men to your banner but you know that these won't be hardened veterans who'll have experienced many successful campaigns and battles. Most of them will be virgin soldiers, not knowing what to expect and unable to defeat a smaller but fiercer and determined army, led by experienced generals who know well the terrain on which they'll be fighting. Even if you won the battle, you'll have suffered serious casualties so that many may question your ability to lead."

Absalom was clearly concerned as Hushai made this point. Hushai continued.

"No, I have a better plan. Wait until you have been able to gather all Israel to you from the northern most town in the territory of Dan to the southern outskirts of the kingdom in Beersheba. Then, at the head of a huge army, you will be able to attack David and his small band of men and utterly destroy David and all who follow him. Even if he takes refuge in a city, he won't be safe for you'll be able to tear down the city ramparts and capture David. Then, you'll be able to lead this victorious army back to Jerusalem, amid the praise and adulation you'll receive from your people." [86]

Hushai had used the right tactics. He'd played on the fears of those with Absalom and appealed to Absalom's pride. So it was, Absalom and those with him agreed that Hushai's advice was better than Ahithophel's. Ahithophel realised that following Hushai's advice would cause disaster to fall on Absalom. In anticipation of what would be the ultimate outcome for himself, he returned to his own home, put his affairs in order and committed suicide by hanging himself.[87]

Hushai let Zadok and Abiathar know how the meeting had gone and urged them to get news to David as soon as possible, telling him to move on from his camp by the Jordan fords to some new site. Zadok and Abiathar had arranged for their sons, Jonathan and Ahimaaz, to be the messengers to convey news to David and had wisely advised them to stay out of Jerusalem where their movements would be observed and reported on to Absalom. Zadok and Abiathar sent the message to their sons staying at En Rogel, just outside Jerusalem, by a servant girl who delivered a letter informing them of what had taken place in Jerusalem and what they should now do.[88]

Jonathan and Ahimaaz set off to inform David, but they realised that they had been observed by one of Absalom's servants. Although this man didn't know who they were, he would take back news to Absalom that a letter had been carried out to two men who were strangers in the area. Absalom would immediately send out a party to follow them. As their pursuers would be on horseback, they would catch up and overtake Ahimaaz and Jonathan, long before they reached David.

"Do you think the man who watched us will follow the young girl who delivered the letter to discover its source?" asked Jonathan.

"If he does," replied Ahimaaz, "he won't learn much. Our fathers are far too wise to be discovered in this way. No, they would have arranged for the delivery of this letter by working through an anonymous middleman. It won't be possible for Absalom to find any link with our fathers and the girl who bore this letter to us."

Ahimaaz and Jonathan then began to make plans for their journey to David in a way which would throw off any who might be sent to pursue them. Ahimaaz knew of a man called Malcam, and his wife, Hushim, who were firm supporters of David. They lived in a house just outside the town of Bahurim. Ahimaaz suggested that if they could hide at Malcam's house, those who were pursuing them would ride by, discover that they had lost the trail and return empty handed to Jerusalem. Once this party had passed Bahurim on their return journey, Ahimaaz and Jonathan could safely continue to deliver their message to David.

On reaching Bahurim and seeking out Malcam, they explained their predicament and asked if they could be hidden from any pursuers. The man's wife, Hushim, suggested the perfect hiding place. This was down a well in their grounds. Jonathan and Ahimaaz climbed down the well and Hushim covered the opening with a large blanket on which she scattered grain to make it appear that it hadn't been disturbed.

When Absalom's men arrived at Bahurim, they enquired if anyone had seen two men pass through. Hushim told them that the men they were seeking had passed over the nearby brook. The pursuers crossed the brook but couldn't pick up the trail. They assumed the messengers had waded along the brook and had left it at some point, either up or down stream, but there was no way of finding their tracks. They therefore had to return to Jerusalem, having failed in their mission.[88]

After these men had gone, Jonathan and Ahimaaz came out of hiding and set off for David's camp. Many others were now crossing the brook so that their tracks would now have been hidden among many. After a long journey, they finally reached David's camp where they gave him the letter describing the outcome of the meeting which Absalom had held with his advisers. David followed the advice contained in the letter, struck camp and moved on to a new site. He finally reached the city of Mahanaim and made his headquarters there.[89]

Meanwhile, following Hushai's advice, Absalom mustered a large army, and after several days had elapsed, he crossed the Jordan and made his way to where he had believed David to have been encamped but David had long since moved on to Mahanaim. When Absalom approached Mahanaim, David sent out his forces to meet Absalom's army, having divided his forces into three units, one third under the leadership of Joab, one third led by Joab's brother Abishai, and the remaining third under Ittai. David expressed the intention of leading his men into battle himself but his commanders persuaded him not to do so. They explained that the enemy's sole objective would be to kill David. Even if the rest of the army suffered heavy casualties, that loss could be borne provided that David was still alive. David acceded to his commanders' demand. His final instruction to them, which he made in the hearing of the rest of the army, was that they should not harm Absalom. He then took up his position by the city gate to review the troops as they marched out to battle.[90]

The armies met at the forest of Ephraim and not on open land. This suited the forces loyal to David well. Although outnumbered by Absalom's forces, they were more experienced warriors and could take full advantage of this particular terrain to outfight Absalom's army. Benaiah and his regiment of Kerethites and Pelethites fought a particularly successful campaign.

Benaiah's regiment encountered Absalom's troops on terrain which was well out of the thickest part of the forest. They were now occupying part of the forest which consisted of clumps of trees, separated by large tracts of open land. Groups of twenty or so of Absalom's men were sheltered in each of these clumps which appeared to offer protection from the arrows which Benaiah's archers might fire at them. On this part of the front facing Benaiah's regiment, Absalom's soldiers appeared to be armed with clubs, swords and spears without a bowman among them. Benaiah gave orders to his captains of fifty to go and attack the men sheltering in these clumps and arranged for his archers to shoot down any men running across open ground, should they try to make their way from one clump of trees to another to support colleagues under attack from Benaiah's men. The strategy worked well. Absalom's soldiers in each clump of trees were easily defeated as they were outnumbered by the more experienced soldiers in Benaiah's platoons who had been sent out to attack them. Any reinforcements from Absalom's men, sheltering in neighbouring clumps of trees were cut down by a hail of arrows released by Benaiah's archers. Benaiah systematically took out the small forces relying on the shelter of the trees one at a time. Although these served to protect Absalom's men from arrows, they were of no help to them when strong platoons of Benaiah's soldiers arrived to attack them on foot. Soon, the remaining groups, sheltering in these trees realised that they would soon be defeated by Benaiah's soldiers if they remained where they were and they started to retreat into the main forest, hotly pursued by Benaiah's men. Very few of Absalom's men had escaped their pursuers by the time a trumpet call was heard, summoning Joab's forces back to their headquarters.

Indeed, the rest of Absalom's army had been in retreat, right along the remainder of the battle front. When Absalom found himself pursued by a contingent of David's men, he rode away from them into the thickest of the forest but his head became caught in a tree. His mount rode on and he was left hanging there. One of Joab's men observed this and reported it to Joab who reprimanded the man for not killing Absalom outright. The soldier protested that this would have been expressly against the king's orders and whatever Joab paid him, this wouldn't protect him from David's wrath when the matter was reported to him. Joab had no such scruples. He was deeply angry with Absalom whom he felt had betrayed his trust in mounting this rebellion against his father after he had brought about a reconciliation between Absalom and David. Ignoring David's orders, Joab killed Absalom as he struggled, trapped by his head in the tree. He had Absalom's body pulled down and buried under a pile of stones.[91]

Joab then ordered the trumpet to sound, recalling his men from pursuing the fleeing forces of Absalom. Ahimaaz, son of Zadok, who knew nothing of the death of Absalom at that time, asked permission to return to Mahanaim to report the good news of David's force's victory. One could usually tell whether the news was good or bad as soon as a messenger came into sight. Some messengers would be associated with good news while others, with bad tidings. Joab realised that the report of Absalom's death would not be received as good news and refused Ahimaaz's request, giving a Cushite the responsibility of bearing the news to David. Ahimaaz persisted in his request to follow the Cushite to give his version of the news. Once Joab estimated that the Cushite was far enough ahead to get to David first, he gave Ahimaaz permission to go. Ahimaaz was a fast runner and knew of a short cut back to the city which enabled him to overtake the Cushite who was following a much longer route.

David and his servants were watching out for a messenger bringing them news of the outcome of the battle. Ahimaaz was the first messenger to come into sight and general relief was felt for Ahimaaz was a messenger who would be associated with good news. A breathless Ahimaaz arrived to report that the king's troops had won a victory.

"What of the young man, Absalom?" asked David. "Is he safe?"

"There seemed to be great confusion going on around Joab just before he sent me with the news of victory, and I have no definite knowledge of what has happened to Absalom."

Just then, the Cushite messenger arrived on the scene and repeated Ahimaaz's news that a great victory had been one. When asked about the fate of Absalom, the Cushite replied,

"May all the king's enemies and any who rise up against him end up like that young man."[92]

The king then realised that Absalom was dead and left the gateway where he had been waiting to welcome the returning troops to vent his grief at Absalom's death.

The victorious troops returned to the city but came in quietly on learning that David would not be there to greet them because he was mourning the death of his son, Absalom.

Joab was furious when he discovered the behaviour of the king.

"You're behaving as if Absalom's life was the only one that mattered and you care nothing for the brave men who have risked their lives, not just to keep you safe but the rest of your family too. It would appear that you would be quite happy to see all your brave servants dead, provided Absalom was still alive. If you don't acknowledge the victory your men have won for you, there'll be wholesale desertion and you'll find yourself in a worse position than you've ever experienced before in your life."

David appreciated the sense of Joab's words so he returned to the city gate to acknowledge the success of his army as they marched before him performing the expected victory parade. The king then made plans to return to Jerusalem. In view of Joab's disobedience in killing Absalom, David appointed Amasa, Joab's cousin, to become commander of the army in place of Joab, even though Amasa had formerly been Absalom's general!

Chapter 12

Shimei and Sheba

Now that Absalom was dead and David restored as undisputed king, the political situation had taken on a new perspective. David had the wholehearted support of the tribe of Judah, but some uncertainty existed among the other tribes, particularly members of the tribe of Benjamin who had been closely related to Saul. Some of them still felt that accession to the throne should have come to a descendent of Saul rather than pass to David but others were pragmatic and recognised that David was now in control. In particular, Shimei, who had publicly cursed David as he fled from Absalom, came and prostrated himself before David, admitted that he had been seriously out of order in hurling abuse at David's men and, as a leading member of the northern tribes of Israel, pledged their support to David.

Memories of the days when Shimei and his men had hurled abuse at David and his army as they passed through Shimei's land still rankled with the senior officers of David's army and Joab's younger brother, Abishai, called for the execution of Shimei for the part he had played during Absalom's rebellion.[98] David rejected Abishai's request. To consolidate his position as king of all Israel, David had to show mercy to any member of the northern tribes who were now pledged to offer him support. He therefore made an oath, promising Shimei that he would not be put to death because of his earlier hostility.[94]

Not all the leading members of the northern tribes were prepared to immediately come out in support of David. Sheba, another Benjaminite, gathered an army of disgruntled Israelites and set himself up in opposition to David. David sent Amasa, the general who had replaced Joab as commander of David's army,[95] to gather a force from the tribe of Judah to track down and defeat Sheba's forces. Amasa took longer than David was prepared to wait to gather his forces so David commissioned Abishai to pursue and hunt down Sheba before he could muster support from powerful, fortified cities in the north of the country. Abishai, supported by Benaiah's elite regiment of Kerethites and Pelethites, set out in pursuit of Sheba.[96]

When Abishai's force reached Gibeon, they were met by Amasa and the men he had gathered. Joab, whom Amasa had replaced as commander in chief, went out to greet Amasa in an apparently friendly fashion, but on meeting him, he stabbed Amasa with a concealed dagger while he was off guard, killing him outright.[97] Joab then took back command of the army from his younger brother, Abishai, and they continued in their pursuit of Sheba who had made his headquarters, the walled city of Abel Beth Maacah. Joab's forces besieged the city. The city could not have held out. It was not well provisioned in anticipation of having to withstand this siege, especially against a commander like Joab. He was experienced in siege warfare and equipped with techniques which would enable him to breach the city walls.

Recognising the danger to her city, which had a reputation for being peaceful, a wise woman from the city came out to negotiate with Joab. When it was established that Joab had no argument with the city but only with Sheba who had rebelled against David and who had taken refuge in the city, the wise woman promised Joab that Sheba's head would be thrown to him from the city walls the next day. The citizen's of Abel Beth Maacah had no desire to suffer in a dispute which was not their own and wisely heeded the advice this this woman gave when she returned to the city. They beheaded Sheba, and as the woman had promised Joab, his head was thrown to him from the city walls. The mission of David's army had been accomplished. Joab had the trumpet blown to signify the end of this campaign and the men dispersed, returning to their own homes.

Chapter 13

Abishag and Eglah

Meanwhile, in Jerusalem, David was re-establishing his authority. The members of David's harem whom Absalom had taken for himself were sent away from the palace to another house, placed under guard, and forbidden to leave this building. Abishag was appalled when she heard what was happening to these unfortunate women through no fault of their own. To start with, they'd been conscripted into the harem without the option of refusal and had no power to resist Absalom's takeover of the harem which was the reason for their present predicament. Some of Abishag's friends, including Rephalah and Shua, were members of this harem and she'd often visited them when they resided in David's palace. Abishag sought out Eglah, the mistress of David's concubines, to discuss the situation in which the concubines now found themselves.

During her early days in Jerusalem, Abishag had made a point of keeping out of Eglah's way to avoid being conscripted into David's harem herself. This danger had long ceased to exist since becoming officially betrothed to Benaiah. Eglah was a short dumpy woman. She wasn't particularly beautiful and didn't have the appearance of the sort of woman one might expect to be a member of David's harem. Being a person working in an official capacity for the royal household, Eglah was very smartly dressed, the embroideries on her tunic being conspicuous as a result of the liberal amount of gold thread worked into the designs. She was intelligent and a good manager and had proved herself as the ideal person to be mistress of David's harem. Once there was no longer any possibility that she could be recruited to David's harem, Abishag had got to know Eglah through her regular visits to her friends in the harem. Abishag had found that Eglah was an agreeable and sensible person and she decided to pay her a visit.

Eglah explained, "These women are effectively under house arrest although they haven't done anything wrong. They were agreeable to becoming members of the harem when I recruited them and for the most part, they've been happy. There was nothing they could do to prevent Absalom taking over the harem when David deserted the city, and even then, very few of them had had any sort of physical relationship with Absalom."

"What's happening to them now is absolutely monstrous," protested Abishag. "Is there anything that can be done to alleviate their situation? What are the main problems they are facing?"

"They complain of boredom, but this is nothing new," Eglah informed Abishag. "This problem is most keenly felt by the more intelligent girls. Those that have just had babies are busy and happy enough but a time arrives when the children have to be fostered out. Before being confined to this house, the mothers were periodically allowed to go out to visit their children in the company of a chaperone. Now, they usually see their children on the occasions when these children have first spent time with David, their father. Then they come to this house. Sadly, David shows very little interest in the children of the harem girls, even though he's their father. The little interest he does show in his children is largely reserved for those who are born to his official wives and these live with their mothers in the main part of the palace.

Now, the mothers in the harem aren't allowed out to visit their children. Since we've been in this new building, the foster parents haven't brought the children here to see their mothers, even though they may have taken them to the palace to see David! Should any foster parents fail to bring the children to the palace to see David after being summoned to do so, a messenger would call round, accompanied by two soldiers. Invariably, after being so prompted, these foster parents would bring their children to the palace within the next couple of days."

Abishag took all this in and answered,

"I think I'll be able to arrange for the foster parents to bring their children to this harem home. Benaiah, my betrothed, is commander of the Kerethites and Pelethites," she proudly stated. "If I ask Benaiah, he'll provide the armed escort to accompany any messenger sent to summon foster parents to bring their children to see their mothers. But tell me about the younger children. Are they catered for?"

"Oh yes." said Eglah. "If nothing else, we're certainly provided with all the material comforts and anything else we need. Over the years, we've collected plenty of nursery equipment. The toddlers are well catered for. Also, I've set aside a couple of rooms to function as a maternity unit. I'm a trained midwife and I can get help from other midwives in the city if needed. Plenty of help is always available from the girls in the harem too. Two of the girls are currently pregnant. The baby due any time now will be David's child but the other girl is only three months pregnant. This baby is almost certainly Absalom's."

"You identified boredom as a main problem facing these women," added Abishag.

"Yes, this causes the girls to get fractious and then they start quarrelling. I have to spend a lot of time acting as peacemaker and on occasions, I've had to be quite a diplomat."

"I think there are things that can be done to alleviate this problem," continued Abishag. "Are any of them musicians, or do they have good singing voices? They could form a choir. Also, I see that there's a significant piece of land in the walled off area around the house. It's never been cultivated so creating a garden would be a challenge which any with horticultural interests might consider taking up."

"Sounds a good idea. There's a lady gardener who works at the palace. She's a friend of mine. I'll get her to bring along some gardening kit and ask her to give some basic instruction for the girls. None of the girls will have done gardening before," said Eglah.

"Will the ladies think gardening an unladylike activity?" ventured Abishag.

"Certainly not," replied Eglah. "They'll be glad of anything to break the monotony of having nothing constructive to do."

Eglah was now getting quite excited about the prospect of introducing practical diversions into the harem house.

"At present, we're given any clothes we wish for," continued Eglah, "but I think some of the girls would enjoy making their own clothes. I know someone who could set them off on this."

Abishag came up with more suggestions.

"Painting, basket making, weaving using yarn they have spun themselves are all suitable activities for ladies and could all be set up in the harem. Men are so lucky in having so many more things they can turn their hand to but there's no reason why women shouldn't be able to do some of these things too. Pottery, simple woodwork like carving, writing and telling stories. Not all these activities will appeal to all the girls but from these ideas and others you might think up, there should be something for everyone to take up to relieve an otherwise boring life."

"Yes, yes," enthused Eglah. "Thank you so much for dropping by to share these thoughts. I hope to be able to get some of these things running fairly soon. I know that you often used to visit your friends in the harem when we were accommodated in the palace. Do continue to visit us in our new home."

Abishag had every intention of doing so and over the next few weeks, she visited her friends, specially Rephalah and Shua whom she had known since they were quite young girls together at Ziklag. She was delighted to see how many of her suggestions had been put into effect by Eglah. The harem was being transformed from being a bunch of languid, disagreeable women into a group of cheerful, active young ladies, busily involved in constructive activities which they were really enjoying.

Chapter 14

Further War with the Philistines

It now appeared that David was securely established in his kingdom. There didn't seem to be any immediate threat or danger. A large part of the army had been stood down. Benaiah and Abishag had agreed that once Benaiah could be discharged from the army, they would marry. Benaiah didn't want to burden his wife with being continuingly anxious for his safety when away from home during the extended campaigns in which the army was frequently involved. They started to draw up marriage plans, not just the wedding ceremony but where they should live and what occupation Benaiah should take up when a civilian.

Sadly, their plans had to be shelved. News reached Jerusalem that a large Philistine army had set out from Ekron and was marching on Jerusalem. The Israelite army was rapidly remobilised. Benaiah gathered his regiment of Kerethites and Pelethites. They set out to meet this foe. The battle was long and drawn out. David, who had gone out with his men, was now showing signs of aging. As the battle wore on he became visibly exhausted and would not have been able to survive an encounter which involved single combat.

From his position along the front, about twenty yards from where David was located not far from Abishai, one of David's senior commanders, Benaiah caught sight of a huge, well-armed giant, bearing down on David. Benaiah called out to Abishai whose attention was fully engaged on marshalling and encouraging his own men,

"Abishai, see to the king, he's in danger!"

Abishai looked to his left and saw this formidable soldier rapidly getting close to David. He was armed with a huge spear and a new sword. It was later discovered that this fearsome warrior was one, Ishbi Benob, a descendent of Rapha and therefore, a relation of Goliath whom David had killed when no more than a boy in his first military encounter. Ishbi Benob had sworn he would kill David and now the opportunity had come up. Abishai managed to intervene between Ishbi Benob and David just in time, deflecting the spear thrust being delivered towards David with his shield. Then followed an epic encounter. Although Ishbi Benob managed to wound Abishai, Abishai was the more skilful fighter and finally delivered a lethal blow to this giant.[99]

The battle was inconclusive and the two armies separated to regroup. In the council of war which followed, David's senior officers insisted that he should no longer go out to fight with them. At his age, he was highly vulnerable. This was clear from the most recent encounter. Should David fall in battle, a terrible blow would be dealt to the morale of the Israelites. David reluctantly accepted this decision.[100]

The Israelite and Philistine armies met again at Gob. Prominent in the Philistine lines were three more giants, descendants of Rapha and therefore, closely related to Goliath. Indeed, one of these, Goliath's nephew was actually called Goliath himself. This time, the battle went decidedly in favour of the Israelites. The three giants were killed in separate encounters with heroes from David's army. The second Goliath was actually killed by Abishag and Zalmon's father, Elhanan. The Philistines retreated and never again challenged Israelite supremacy in the land.[109]

Chapter 15

David's Last Days

Now, surely Benaiah could resign his commission and be free to marry Abishag but again, no. Another situation had arisen which required their wedding to be delayed. The most recent campaign had clearly taken its toll on David's health. He was now increasingly frail and continuously complaining of feeling cold. It was obvious to those around him that he hadn't long left to live. He had now reached the stage when he would need round the clock nursing but to whom could this job be assigned. Not anyone would do. Although she wouldn't be required to become the king's mistress, the woman recruited would need to be not only beautiful but a virgin. The king would not have happily come under the care of a middle-aged matron, however motherly and competent she may have been. Abishag was an obvious choice. She was beautiful. She was known to the king. She was known to be chaste, but she was engaged to Benaiah.

Nathan and Hushai arranged to meet Benaiah and Abishag to assess their reaction.

"David has only weeks, maybe days, to live," explained Nathan. "We want to make his last days as comfortable as possible for him. He's asking for female company, not from one of his harem, he's well past anything like that, but a presentable person just to provide nursing. The lady needed would be expected to keep the king's mind alert with intelligent conversation and up to date with whatever's going on in Jerusalem. While someone from his harem might have appeared to be the obvious choice, the restrictions he has placed on these women make this impossible and in any case, we can't see anyone in the harem who would be up to the task anyway. We're sure that none of his official wives would be prepared or even capable of fulfilling this duty, some of his wives being almost as old as David anyway. You, Abishag, are the only name we have come up with as a person with the necessary qualities to fulfil this role. You have the intelligence, the compassion and a caring attitude. Through your relationship with Benaiah, you are conversant with all that goes on around the king. You, have the further quality of beauty which is something we know David will expect of anyone attending to him in this role."

A period of embarrassed silence followed. Benaiah looked at Abishag. Abishag looked back at Benaiah. Nathan and Hushai patiently waited for a response.

"Did you describe David's life expectancy as no more than weeks, perhaps only days?" asked Abishag.

"Who can be certain of how long a person may live?" replied Hushai, "but I've seen many in the same state that David is now. I know that his days are numbered. David's mind is lucid and he knows what's going on around him but I think it's only his determination which is keeping him alive. He needs to be kept alive to enable the question of his successor to be resolved. David will name his successor and if he makes a bad choice, that will be a disaster for the kingdom. Solomon would be our choice, and we think that the king has also decided that he should be the next king of Israel. However, he has not publicly made this known. The role you play now, Abishag, could be crucial to the future of Israel. We can't allow all that has been achieved in David's reign to be lost."

As Abishag continued to contemplate the situation, her mind settled on the king's eldest son, Adonijah, and she inwardly shuddered when she thought back to the lewd advances he had made to her in the past, and indeed, still did, should they happen to meet during the normal course of the day's events. He mustn't be allowed to become king.

Abishag finally looked up and gave the answer Nathan and Hushai had hoped for.

"Yes, for the sake of the kingdom and of course, in the interests of David's wellbeing, I am prepared to do what you ask."

Nathan and Hushai showed obvious signs of relief at this point.

"BUT," continued Abishag, "I am betrothed to Benaiah and therefore, this must be a joint decision. Benaiah, are you prepared to delay our wedding so that I can fulfil this service to the king and thereby, help safeguard the nation's future?"

Benaiah now felt himself put on the spot but his overriding concern was for Abishag and what she wanted.

"If you are prepared to do this, Abishag," he replied, "then do so with my blessing. The future of Israel is of importance to all of us."

"So it was that Abishag moved in to nurse David during his final days on earth.[102] Apart from Hushai, Zadok, Nathan and Benaiah, he had few other visitors during this time. The only wives who visited David were Abigail and Bathsheba. Three days after Abishag had taken up her duties, David asked to specially see

Bathsheba. Abishag paid great attention to their conversation.

"I have been so pleased to see the way your son, our son, Solomon has developed," David said to Bathsheba. "Of all my sons, he alone has demonstrated a really responsible attitude to his position as the son of a king. I know that this is largely due to the sensible way in which you have brought him up and I know that my most trusted councillors have had a hand in this too. It is therefore my intention to nominate him as my successor."[103]

Bathsheba beamed with pleasure at this statement and bowed low before David.

"You honour me and my son in a way which exceeds our wildest expectations. It is important that you let your councillors know this at the earliest opportunity," Bathsheba wisely added.

David summoned Nathan, Zadok, Hushai and Benaiah to join them and made his intention known to them. Anticipating the effect this decision would have on his sons and his other wives, he asked them not to make this decision public just yet. At that point, David sank back on the cushions which supported him. A look of contentment replaced the anxious expression which had previously marked his face.

Over the next few days, David's health deteriorated further and it was clear the end was near. This prompted a reaction which was the last thing David's special councillors wanted. Adonijah, declared himself to be king. Preceded by fifty men he had chosen, he rode out of Jerusalem in his chariot, to En Rogel, just outside Jerusalem. There, he sacrificed a large number of sheep and cattle at a nearby altar and invited many of the royal officials and his brothers to a banquet he was putting on to celebrate his becoming king in succession to David. Among the senior officials Adonijah invited as his principal supporters were Abiathar, the priest, and Joab, the army commander. Conspicuous by their absence were Nathan, Zadok, Benaiah, Hushai and Solomon. Adonijah was well aware of where their sympathies lay and didn't invite them to this premature celebration. Cries of 'long live the king' were heard from the room where this banquet was being held.

News soon reached Nathan of what was going on. He immediately contacted Bathsheba to put her in the picture. He told her to report what was happening to David. Nathan assured Bathsheba that he would shortly follow her in to provide independent confirmation of this untoward event. Bathsheba came into the room where the king was being read to by Abishag. Bathsheba was in a state of some distress. She reminded the king of his promise that Solomon should be his successor and described to him what Adonijah was now doing. Bathsheba declared through her tears,

"As king, Adonijah will execute me and your son, Solomon."

No sooner had Bathsheba finished speaking than Nathan entered the royal presence to confirm everything Bathsheba had said.[104]

Frail as he was, this news galvanised the king into action. He summoned Benaiah, Zadok and Hushai gave them instructions that they should send out trumpeters throughout Jerusalem to declare that Solomon was the new king. David reminded them that making Solomon his successor as king over Judah and Israel was a pledge he had made during an earlier meeting at which they had been present. This reminder was unnecessary. They were well aware of David's pledge.

Bathsheba knelt before David now looking relieved that events would take a turn in the right direction.

"May my Lord, King David, live forever," she declared.[105]

Of course, she didn't mean this in terms of David's earthly life but was expressing a desire for him to join his illustrious forefathers, Abraham, Isaac and Israel in heaven.

Benaiah then spoke,

"May the Lord our God confirm what the king has wished. As the Lord has been with David, so may he be with Solomon to make his throne even greater than that of his father, David."[106]

The next hour was action-packed. Trumpeters were sent through Jerusalem proclaiming that David had nominated Solomon as the next king. The news was rapturously received by the citizens.

Benaiah organised the procession to conduct Solomon to Gihon where the Tabernacle was located. Here, Zadok would anoint Solomon. The procession was led by Benaiah as commander of the King's bodyguard. He was followed by the Kerethites, marching three abreast. Then came Solomon, mounted on King David's mule and accompanied by Zadok, Nathan and Hushai. The other half of the King's Bodyguard, the Pelethites, brought up the rear. They marched to what was then the equivalent of a regimental band but this just consisted of trumpets and drums, the trumpets playing a marching tune to the regular beat of the drums.

News had quickly spread round the city and the procession was followed by cheering crowds, making their way to the Tabernacle, the site where the anointing would take place.[107]

The ceremony was completed. This was marked by a long blast on a trumpet and a great cry went up, "Long live the King!"

Meanwhile, at Adonijah's feast, the sound of a great commotion and trumpet blasts could be heard. Everyone was wondering whatever was going on? Joab felt that he in particular should know of anything happening in the city of sufficient magnitude to create such a disturbance. His ignorance was short lived. Abiathar's son, Jonathan, arrived with news. Jonathan was a messenger associated with good news but this time, the news wasn't good from the standpoint of those gathered with Adonijah. Jonathan declared that David had made Solomon his successor as king and he had now been anointed to confirm his status. Solomon had been accompanied to his anointing by the Kerethites and Pelethites and the crowds were wild with jubilation at David's choice. Solomon was now seated on the royal throne and was being congratulated by all the officials who serve the king at the palace.

Fearing that they might be rounded up by Benaiah's soldiers, the guests at Adonijah's banquet panicked and quickly dispersed. Realising that he himself was in danger in view of his precipitate action in prematurely declaring himself to be king, Adonijah made his way to the Tabernacle which was now deserted as the anointing of Solomon had taken place some time earlier. He went in and grasped the horns of the altar, indicating that he had taken sanctuary in this most holy place of the nation of Israel.[108]

Chapter 16

Solomon Consolidates his New Status

Now that the kingdom was sufficiently powerful to be secure from attack by neighbouring tribes, and a good king was on the throne, now was surely a time that Benaiah and Abishag could go ahead and make concrete plans for their marriage. Benaiah, in his role as leader of the king's bodyguard, would have a few more duties to perform first to firmly establish Solomon's position as Israel's new king.

Solomon was well aware of the main threats to his security and he was ruthless in eliminating these potential dangers. First, there was the would-be king, Adonijah who had already demonstrated that as eldest of David's sons, he considered that he had an automatic right to succeed to the throne. Solomon arranged for Benaiah to send men from his bodyguard to bring Adonijah to him but they returned to Solomon without him. They told the king that Adonijah had taken sanctuary in the Tabernacle and would not come away unless Solomon assured him that he would not put him to death. Solomon thought carefully and then stated,

"No harm will come to Adonijah if he proves himself to be a worthy man but should he do the slightest thing to threaten our security, he will surely be put to death."

The soldiers returned to the Tabernacle with this message and brought Adonijah into Solomon's presence where the king repeated this assurance and curtly sent Adonijah back to his home.

Had Adonijah been prepared to passively accept the status quo, all would have been well for him but he wasn't a prudent man. He decided that the safest way to communicate with Solomon was through his mother so he went to Bathsheba and asked her to request Solomon that he might be allowed to marry Abishag the Shunammite. There was more to this request than might meet the eye. It was the practice in those days for someone with aspirations to be king to take over his predecessor's harem. Absalom had done just such a thing at the start of his rebellion. Without knowing the entirely chaste relationship which had existed between David and Abishag, Adonijah had wrongly assumed that Abishag was a new member of David's harem, now that the previous harem had been sent into isolation. To use the style, 'Abishag the Shunammite' based on Abishag's city of origin was not an acceptable way to refer to her for now she expected to be described as 'Abishag betrothed to Benaiah'. Adonijah had paid a great insult to Abishag and Benaiah in making this request and by referring to her in a way which disregarded her relationship with Benaiah. He had made a serious error of judgement.

Solomon was furious when Bathsheba brought this request to him because he was aware of the message that would be conveyed to the people if Adonijah married someone believed to be part of David's harem. Solomon immediately gave Benaiah orders to take an execution squad to Adonijah's home and execute him. Benaiah duly fulfilled this grisly duty. While Benaiah and Abishag themselves would not have wanted Adonijah to pay with his life for his indiscretion, Benaiah and Abishag held Adonijah in low regard. With Adonijah's demise, Abishag would no longer have to dread being subject to lewd comments whenever she came across or met Adonijah.[109]

Abiathar and Joab were two senior members of David's council who had supported Adonijah and posed a serious threat to Solomon. Abiathar was summoned to come before Solomon who informed him that he deserved to die for conspiring with Adonijah to make himself king. However, in view of his previous loyal service, especially as a custodian of that most holy symbol, the Ark, his punishment was to be removed from the priesthood and exiled from Jerusalem.[110] This sentence might be regarded as the fulfilment of a prophecy made many years earlier by Samuel against the descendants of Eli, a former chief priest[111]. So it was, Zadok became high priest in place of Abiathar.

When Joab heard what had happened to Abiathar, he realised that his own life was in danger and as Adonijah had done earlier, he sought sanctuary by entering the Tabernacle and grasping the horns of the altar.

While his conspiracy with Adonijah would have been deemed a sufficient crime to merit the death sentence, Joab had committed other very serious crimes from which he had evaded punishment. In order to safeguard his own position as commander of the army, he had murdered Abner and Amasa, two other generals. These were worthy men of great nobility whom David would have preferred to Joab as the commander of his army. These acts of murder were all the more heinous because Joab had approached his victims with the pretence of coming in friendship. He would have claimed that killing Abner, who had earlier killed Joab's brother, Asahel, in battle, was to settle a blood feud but no such excuse could be given for murdering Amasa. Joab had also killed Absalom, contrary to King David's orders, and had been complicit with David in the murder of Uriah. Joab was not a good man and clearly deserved his fate!

Benaiah was again sent out with his execution squad and commanded Joab to come out of the Tabernacle. Joab had refused and told Benaiah to come into the Tabernacle and kill him there. This was something Benaiah was reluctant to do. Unless he was overruled by a higher authority, he would not violate the rules of sanctuary and returned to Solomon to explain why he hadn't fulfilled his order. Solomon reissued his order, pointing out that as Joab himself had asked Benaiah to execute him in the Tabernacle, this would not violate sanctuary. Benaiah and his execution squad duly carried out the king's order.[112]

These tasks complete, surely now Abishag and Benaiah could go ahead with their planned nuptials, but no, another quite unexpected obstacle arose. Now that the former commander of the army had been executed, Solomon told Benaiah that he was to be the next army supremo.[113] How could he now resign his commission in the army? He returned home to discuss the new situation with Abishag. This promotion was a mixed blessing. While at the outset of his military career, Benaiah could never have dreamed of being the general in charge of the whole of Israel's army, the arrangement he had made with Abishag was that they shouldn't get married until he had left the army to spare Abishag any anxiety about his safety when he had been called away to fight. Abishag was prepared to marry

Benaiah, even if he did remain a soldier but they consulted with Nathan who could always be relied upon to give wise advice when situations like this arose.

Nathan's counsel was very reassuring. He told Benaiah and Abishag that he had expected Benaiah to rise to this position once Solomon had become king and he had prayed into what the future might hold. His prophetic insight had reinforced something which was becoming self-evident, that Israel was now so powerful and firmly established in the land that during Solomon's reign, the kingdom would not be seriously threatened from without. Nathan therefore gave welcome advice to Benaiah and Abishag.

"The reason you both delayed getting married while Benaiah was still in the army, was because of the danger involved by any following that profession. Benaiah wanted you, Abishag, to be spared the anxiety faced by any army wife while her husband is in danger away fighting. However, in the immediate future, this danger no longer exists. Israel is so powerful and secure that none will dare to rise up against this nation. However, to maintain that peace and security, the nation needs a strong army. There is no-one more suitable than yourself, Benaiah, to take control of the army. You have the experience to maintain the army in such a state of preparedness that none will ever challenge Israel while you're in charge of its forces. I think therefore that you may confidently go ahead with your marriage with every prospect of many long and happy years ahead."

So it was that Benaiah took charge of Israel's armed forces. One other domestic duty came up for Benaiah to fulfil before the day set for the wedding.

Solomon was aware that a potential challenge to his kingship might come from the northern tribes of Israel who still felt loyal to the memory of Saul who had been their king and champion. The Benjamite leader who just might foster a rebellion among the northern tribes was Shimei who had insulted David and his troops as they fled from Jerusalem during Absalom's rebellion. Although Shimei had made peace with David, David was now a past king. Would Shimei be prepared to accept Solomon as the new king? Solomon was not going to risk any problem from that quarter. Shimei had to be located away from any potential power base. Solomon sent for Shimei and demanded that he should build a house for himself in Jerusalem and that he should never leave the city. To do so would be to invite a death sentence. Shimei agreed to Solomon's demand and set himself up in Jerusalem. Shimei felt relieved that the restrictions which had been placed on himself were so limited. He had expected a far greater punishment for his disloyalty to David on Solomon's accession to the throne.

Once Shimei was settled and felt sure that he was no longer regarded as a threat, a situation arose which led to Shimei breaking his promise to remain in Jerusalem. Two of his slaves fled from him to seek their freedom in Gath. Shimei left Jerusalem to recover these slaves and Solomon got to hear of this. On Shimei's return, Solomon sent Benaiah to Shimei's house with his execution party. Benaiah retained unpleasant memories of being stoned by Shimei's men as he fled Jerusalem with David at the time of Absalom's rebellion. Shimei had no defence against the charge that he had disregarded the arrangement he had made with Solomon and had left the city. Thus, Benaiah carried out another execution to rid the nation from the remaining internal threat to its security.[114] Fulfilling the role of royal executioner was not one which Benaiah cherished. If killing had to be carried out, Benaiah would have preferred it to be in the heat of battle. However, in view of the senior military position he now held, Benaiah had no alternative but to carry out the king's orders. The requirement that anyone serving in the military has to obey orders, regardless of their morality, has often led to soldiers having to carry out deeds which they regard as distasteful or even unethical. In such cases, a defence which may justifiably be made by a soldier accused of wrong-doing is that he was just obeying orders.

With the nation in an unprecedented state of security, surely, now the wedding which had been planned could go ahead.

Chapter 17

The Wedding

Benaiah and Abishag went together to Solomon to announce their plans for getting married. An officer of Benaiah's seniority didn't need to go through any formal ceremony to be admitted into the presence of the king. Solomon was delighted to hear this news of two people who, in their different ways, had given such special service to the kingdom, both to David, and more recently to himself. He congratulated them and offered to make them a special wedding present. He asked, what would they like?

This offer was most unexpected. Caught on the spot like this, Benaiah had no idea of what would be an appropriate thing to request but Abishag had a clear idea.

"When, after Absalom's rebellion, David authorised that the members of his harem should be restricted to live in a house which they were not permitted to leave," she started, "they were sentenced to remain under house arrest for life but he didn't specify whose life.[118] David is now dead and therefore, to my way of thinking, the women in the harem are now technically widows and no longer bound by David's edict.

However, they're still held under guard at that house. If you wish to give us a gift, we would dearly love to see these ladies released from house arrest."

Solomon displayed the wisdom for which he became reputed and immediately agreed to grant this request. He further promised to make money available to help them get resettled. In view of the way Solomon's marital affairs developed during his reign, he may have been thinking even then of the accommodation that would be needed for his own harem. This house would then be a useful resource.

"In view of the very unselfish nature of this request," Solomon added, "I have another gift in mind which I would like you to accept. Shimei, who has now been executed, had considerable estates in the northern part of my kingdom. There are many in that part of the country who would still prefer to be ruled by a king descended from Saul. The Benjaminites, led by another trouble-maker, may well rebel to achieve this end, just as Shimei was on the point of doing. A powerful man like yourself, controlling what was Shimei's territory, would be a considerable safeguard against such a rebellion taking place. Will you therefore accept Shimei's lands and estates as a wedding present from a king who is grateful for all that you have done?"

This was a gift which Benaiah and Abishag gladly accepted for up until that time, they were not among the rich of the land, relying entirely on Benaiah's salary as a soldier.

They left the palace and made their way to the harem house and were surprised to discover that Solomon's order had already been transmitted to the guards and the women were making preparation to leave. Solomon was not one to hang about when an executive decision or action was required. The women were in a state of some excitement. Eglah greeted her friend, Abishag, as she arrived. In spite of her position of seniority in the harem which would now no longer exist, Eglah too was glad to be leaving the building. The job she had carried out so well had not been without stress and Eglah had really had enough. Abishag asked if they could see her special friends in the harem, Rephalah and Shua. In spite of the new situation which now existed, Eglah was still not sure whether men could enter the harem house and she sent for Rephalah and Shua to come out and meet Benaiah and Abishag.

Abishag recounted in some detail what had been said during their audience with Solomon. She told Eglah, Rephalah and Shua of the plans that Benaiah and herself were making to get married and hoped that they would be prepared to be bridesmaids. Of course, they were. The women hugged each other and were all in a state of some euphoria. Benaiah and Abishag left their friends to carry on with their packing and made their way home to proceed with the arrangements for their own nuptials.

The first ritual to be arranged was the **Mikvah**. The literal meaning of mikvah is water in a pool or container set aside for a ritual of purification. In preparation for the wedding ceremony, the bride is immersed in the pool and as she emerges, she is considered to have been transferred from the old life as a single woman to a new life as a married woman. The ritual symbolises a change in her status as she moves from the authority of her father to that of her husband. Words which are often spoken during this ceremony by the presiding priest or rabbi are,

"Before whom do you purify yourself? None other than your Father in Heaven. Just as the water of the mikvah purifies you from impurity, so does the Holy One purify Israel. Blessed be his name."

After the mikvah, it was traditional for the groom's father to prepare a wedding chamber for his son and wife at his own house. This could have taken as long as a year, giving the bride adequate time to get herself prepared to leave her own parent's house as she went to live with her new husband in their marital home. The situation for Benaiah and Abishag was rather different. Being older, they had already bought what was to become their marital home and this was where Benaiah now lived. There would be a much shorter lead up time to the actual wedding. During this time, Abishag was able to prepare the palanquin *(**Hebrew – aperion**),* a covered litter which would be borne on the shoulders of four attendants to bear her and Benaiah to the bridal home.

Between the mikvah and the wedding ceremony, Abishag had the status of being a consecrated bride and as such, she wore a crown as a symbol of this consecration. It was usual for this crown to be made in the form of a circlet of flowers but Benaiah and Abishag were able to afford something better and Abishag was provided with what was known as a 'Jerusalem of Gold bridal crown'. As the name suggests, this was made of gold and was to become a valuable keepsake.

The next stage in the process involved the bridegroom returning to take the bride to the wedding chamber. This would normally have been a room in the groom's parent's home but Benaiah had prepared the wedding chamber in his own home. It was traditional but not obligatory for the groom to return at an unexpected time late in the evening but Abishag and Benaiah saw no point in following this tradition. In their case, they already had their own home and so were not dependent on Benaiah's father, Jehoiada, requiring them to wait until he declared the bridal chamber was ready. Why keep the wedding guests, musicians and other attendants waiting unnecessarily?

The day of the wedding arrived. Benaiah left the house which was to become their marital abode, preceded by a procession made up of Benaiah's friends and trumpeters crying,

"Behold, the bridegroom is coming, go out to meet him."

Benaiah was smartly dressed in the type of clothes worn by army officers when not on duty. On reaching Abishag's home, she was carried out on the 'aperion' by her attendants and was joined by Benaiah who sat next to her. Abishag was wearing a splendid red wedding dress, exquisitely embroidered with gold thread and reaching to her ankles. She was veiled and part of the ceremony called **bedeken**, involved Benaiah lifting the veil to ensure he was marrying the right bride. On the return to what was to become their marital home, they were accompanied, not just by Benaiah's friends and the trumpeters, but other guests, some of whom were torchbearers who lighted the way through the gathering dusk, additional musicians, including flautists and harpists, and Abishag's five bridesmaids. Chief among the bridesmaids were Atarah, Rephalah and Shua. The bridesmaids carried lamps they had trimmed to provide extra illumination as they followed the 'aperion' for the short journey they were about to make. Although now elderly and somewhat infirm, and only able to contribute to a limited degree to the marriage preparations, Benaiah and Abishag's parents, Jehoida and Jerusha, Elhanan and Acsah, with the help of other relatives proudly joined the procession as they ambled to their son and daughter's new abode.

The next part of the ceremony was called the **Huppah**. It is also known by the more meaningful word, 'hometaking'. On reaching their home, Benaiah alighted from the 'aperion' and went to the door of the house. When he was in place, Abishag left the 'aperion' to be kissed and ceremoniously welcomed by her husband. The pair of them then welcomed the rest of the guests to their home where they sat down for a meal which had already been laid out by the house servants. After the meal, Abishag and Benaiah were conducted to the bridal chamber in the house.

Benaiah had no trouble in identifying Zalmon as the man he wanted to be the 'friend of the bridegroom' (equivalent of today's best man). They had known each other from the day their families had met on their flight from the battle of Gilboa to Ziklag. The valour displayed by Zalmon during the nation's military campaigns had led to him being identified as one of Israel's most illustrious soldiers.[116] Following tradition, Zalmon waited on guard outside the bridal chamber or huppah.

The time spent in the huppah could be as long as seven days while the wedding guests came and went. During this period, food for the wedding guests was in plentiful supply. On entering the huppah, Benaiah and Abishag suddenly found themselves away from the hectic environment of wedding celebration and able to enjoy a time of peace and quiet together. They talked about the plans they had for their future together, the family they hoped to rear, the service Abishag hoped to give to the poorer members of their society and how Benaiah's ongoing army career might impact on their marriage. In due course, Benaiah and Abishag consummated their marriage and Benaiah communicated to his friend waiting outside that he and Abishag were now man and wife in the fullest sense. Zalmon then declared to any present,

"Let us greatly rejoice for Benaiah and Abishag's joy has been fulfilled."

This was the sign for the final stage of the wedding to be completed. The news was spread to any guests who were not in the house at the time and they all regathered to hear the blessings and partake of the feast that followed.

The seven blessings were then read out by Zalmon in a clear confident voice.

1. **Blessed art Thou, O Lord our God, King of the universe, Creator of the fruit of the vine.**
. (As this blessing was read, Zalmon held up a cup of wine.)
2. **Blessed art Thou, O Lord our God, King of the universe, who hast created all things to Thy glory.**
3. **Blessed art Thou, O Lord our God, King of the universe, Creator of man.**
4. **Blessed art Thou, O Lord our God, King of the universe, who hast made man in thine image, after Thy likeness, and hast prepared unto him, out of his very self, a perpetual fabric.**
5. **May she who was barren be exceedingly glad and exult, when her children are**

> gathered within her in joy. Blessed art Thou, O Lord, who makest Zion joyful through her children.
> 6. *O make these loved companions greatly to rejoice, even as of old Thou didst gladden Thy creatures in the Garden of Eden. Blessed art Thou, O Lord, who makest bridegroom and bride to rejoice.*
> 7. *Blessed art Thou, O Lord our God, King of the universe, who hast created joy and gladness, bridegroom and bride, mirth and exultation, pleasure and delight, love, brotherhood, peace and fellowship. Blessed art Thou, O Lord, who makest the bridegroom to rejoice with the bride.*

A second glass of wine was then brought to the couple and Benaiah and Abishag both took a sip. Following tradition, Benaiah then smashed the glass so sealing their marriage covenant. This symbolised that the past was behind them. A new phase of life had begun and life would never be the same again.

This ceremony was followed by the marriage supper which is called a **seudat mitvah.** The origins of this custom whose intent was to instil joy into the bride and bridegroom, originate from the feast put on by Jacob's father-in-law, Laban, at Jacob and Leah's wedding. All the local people were invited. Music was played during this feast and the celebration also involved dancing.

At the end of the feast, the guests dispersed. The long awaited marriage of Benaiah and Abishag was fulfilled. Nine months later, they had a baby son. Today, the child would be called a honeymoon baby. They named him Jehoiada after Benaiah's father. In modern medical parlance, Abishag would be described as an elderly prima gravida. She would have been considered to be well beyond the normal age for people of that day to have their first baby.

As one reflects on this protracted wedding ceremony, one can see how Jesus so aptly described himself as the bridegroom of the church for so much of the symbolism in this typical Israelite marriage ceremony corresponded to events and stories recounted in the gospel. The ritual washing corresponded to baptism. The first cup of wine corresponded to the cup shared at the last supper sealing the new marriage covenant that was made between God and his people which we know as the church. The second cup corresponded to the cup that Jesus said he would drink it new with his disciples in his Father's kingdom.[128] The ring, which reminded the betrothed of the bridegroom she was to marry, corresponded to the Holy Spirit who draws attention, not to himself but to the one who purchased us. Echoes of the Israelite wedding ceremony are found very strongly in the parable of the ten bridesmaids awaiting the return of the bridegroom, not knowing the time he would arrive.[129]

The wedding of Benaiah and Abishag was not completely typical of the traditional Israelite wedding and this was very much due to the fact that they had reached a stage in life where their parents were elderly and they had already bought their own home. In the typical Israelite wedding, the groom would not know when the time was right to go to claim his bride. This was decided by his father. So too, Jesus declared that he did not know when he would return. This was known only by his Father.[117] The coming of the bridegroom will be so sudden that there will be no time to draw close to God unless we have done this already.

> **Matthew ch 24 *v27*** *For as the lightening comes from the east and flashes to the west, so also will the coming of the Son of Man be.*

Will there be a marriage supper? Certainly, this is described in the book of Revelation.

> **Revelation ch 19 v 9** *Blessed are those who are called to the marriage supper of the Lamb.*

The imagery of the wedding is so beautifully expressed in lines from Samuel Stone's hymn, '***The church's one foundation is Jesus Christ, our Lord***'. This hymn had a profound effect on the delegates which attended the Lambeth conference held in 1888..

> '*From heaven he came and sought us to be his holy bride.*
> *With his own blood he bought us and for our life he died.*'

This would be a good point to end this story but a further chapter is needed to explain how the Jewish nation fared during the period that Benaiah and Abishag settled into their married life together.

Chapter 18

The Reign of King Solomon

Benaiah and Abishag split their time between their home in Jerusalem and the estate which had belonged to Shimei in Benjamite territory. The stewards who had been left to administer the estate were more than happy that Benaiah was the new owner. They had always felt insecure when Shimei was in charge with a constant undercurrent of fermenting rebellion against David. Benaiah's reputation had gone before him, not just as a valiant soldier but also, a chivalrous one. The estate proved a valuable refuge for Benaiah and Abishag at times when political intrigue seemed to permeate the capital. Benaiah was a soldier, not a politician, and he saw politics as a dirty game.

As Nathan had prophesied, Israel was territorially secure and during their marriage, Abishag no longer had cause to wait anxiously for the safe return of her husband from a military campaign. Israel's security was very much due to the sound way that Benaiah as commander in chief, developed the army. It was clear that cavalry would be a key to success in any future conflict. In the past, the Israelites had relied mainly on its infantry and there had been occasions when this had been the key to success when confronted by an army equipped with chariots. The defeat of Sisera by the judge, Barak, was such an example.[118] Warfare had now developed and new tactics and new weapons were needed. Benaiah arranged for fine horses to be purchased from Egypt. He had organised the building of stables which could accommodate up to four thousand chariots and their horses, and another set of stables for the cavalry which were large enough to take twelve thousand horses.[119] Benaiah was well known throughout the army as he frequently visited garrison towns to review the state of his troops.

Benaiah's most important military activity during the reign of Solomon was to deal with an internal uprising. Although renowned for his wisdom in dealing with difficult legal cases which were presented before him, Solomon's wisdom did not extend to all aspects of his reign. The internal rebellion was directly the result of what might be described as Solomon's folly.

Solomon fulfilled the task which his father, David, had commanded him to complete. This was the building of the world-famous temple for which David had already left plans. The splendour and furnishings of this beautiful building were absolutely awe inspiring. It took Solomon seven years to complete the building of the temple.[120] He also built himself a magnificent palace which was even larger and more splendid than the one his father David had built. This edifice took thirteen years to complete.[121] The palace needed to be large to accommodate what might be described as Solomon's chief folly. To establish an alliance with the powerful neighbouring kingdom of Egypt, he married Pharaoh's daughter but he didn't restrict his marriage to a single wife. He established alliances with neighbouring kingdoms by taking wives from among their royalty. He also created a harem of concubines but he took many more wives and concubines than even David. In total, he had seven hundred wives of noble descent and three hundred concubines! He was not discerning in his choice of wife but intermarried with the wives of the pagan nations which had occupied the land of Israel and surrounding countries. This was contrary to God's command to the Israelites when they entered the land of Canaan, as it was then called, under the leadership of Joshua. Solomon demonstrated his love for his wives by condoning their religious practices, even to the extent of building places of worship dedicated to these foreign gods and offering sacrifices to them himself.[122]

One of the most able officials in Solomon's kingdom was a young man called Jeroboam.[123] He was a devout young man, well versed in the law and traditions of Israel. Jeroboam could clearly see that Solomon was seriously deviating from what might be expected of a king of Israel, but what could he do about it? Then, one day, as Jeroboam was leaving the capital, he was met by a prophet called Ahijah who was wearing a new cloak. He took Jeroboam to one side and they talked about the actions of Solomon which were detrimental to the faith of Israel. The idolatry into which Solomon was getting involved was absolutely contrary to the teaching and practices that Moses and the patriarchs had given the people of Israel by word and by example, and the Israelites were beginning to copy Solomon's bad example. Ahijah then made a prophecy to Jeroboam which answered this young man's question about what should done to deal with the problem of idolatry in Israel. This was to set Jeroboam on a course of action.

In the dramatic style which characterised the way that Jewish prophets proclaimed what was to happen, Ahijah took his new cloak and tore it into twelve pieces. He gave ten of these to Jeroboam.

"These pieces of cloak," declared Ahijah, "represent the twelve tribes of Israel. Because of Solomon's sin, ten of the tribes will be taken from Solomon and given to you. However, the Lord has told me that this will not happen in Solomon's lifetime. Because of the regard with which God held David and the promise that God made to David and his progeny, Solomon's descendants will retain just two of the tribes of Israel. You will become king of the remaining ten. Provided that you are as faithful as David was in keeping my statutes and commands, God will create for you a dynasty which will be as enduring as that of David."[124]

This message came to Jeroboam well on into Solomon's reign and he decided he would take the necessary action to bring about its fulfilment. He gathered a rebel army from his tribe of Ephraim which he was prepared to lead to take over the kingdom. Benaiah's job as chief of the army was to put down any such rebellion. Solomon wanted Jeroboam killed.

Benaiah's force met with the small army that Jeroboam had gathered. It was clear that Jeroboam's force would be no match for the numerically stronger battle-hardened veterans of Benaiah's army. However, Benaiah didn't want to shed the blood of fellow Israelites unnecessarily and before launching into hostilities, he arranged to meet with Jeroboam in a tent erected between the two forces. No-one knows exactly what passed between them because the negotiations were secret, Benaiah and Jeroboam meeting together alone in the tent. However, the following is most probably the way the discussion went.

Jeroboam described in great detail the prophecy he had received from Ahijah to explain to Benaiah why he was taking this action and raising a rebellion. Benaiah had been as disturbed as Jeroboam at the way Solomon was leading the nation into idolatry but his job as army commander was to ensure the security of the kingdom. However much he sympathised with a cause, his oath to defend Israel meant his prime duty was to put down any rebellion which threatened the state. Benaiah had listened carefully to the prophecy which Jeroboam had recited almost verbatim. If this was a word from God, it would certainly come about. However, Benaiah identified a part of the prophecy of which Jeroboam hadn't properly taken into account, that the kingdom was not to be divided until the reign of Solomon's successor. Jeroboam's rebellion was therefore premature. Benaiah therefore advised Jeroboam to disband his army and take himself into exile in another country where he would be safe until the time was ripe for Ahijah's prophecy to be fulfilled.

Jeroboam was an intelligent man. He was well aware of the disparity in the strength of the forces which now confronted each other. If he was charged with acting to fulfil a prophecy delivered by God to his prophet, it was incumbent on him to adhere to God's timing. The two men left the negotiating tent. Jeroboam returned to his Ephraimite army and explained that there were very good reasons why they needed to await God's timing before taking action. I think that much to his men's relief, for they could see that they were outmatched by Benaiah's force, Jeroboam disbanded his army. He himself went into exile in Egypt where he would be safe until the time was ripe for God's prophecy to be fulfilled.[125]

Benaiah was able to return to Solomon to tell him that the rebellion had been put down. This was much to Solomon's relief. Solomon didn't want to hear the details of any battle that had been fought described. He was just sorry that Jeroboam had escaped but glad he was no longer around to create any further trouble.

By now, Benaiah was well past the age of military service and he resigned his post of commander in chief of the Israelite army. He and Abishag spent their remaining days in retirement, enjoying seeing their son, Jehoiada grow up into the sort of young man of whom they could be truly proud.

Benaiah and Abishag had died before the end of Solomon's forty-year reign and were not around to see the fulfilment of Ahijah's prophecy. Solomon's son and successor, Rehoboam, was a pig-headed, arrogant young man who didn't have the wisdom to sensibly negotiate with Jeroboam when he returned from exile in Egypt to fulfil Ahijah's prophecy. Thus, the kingdom was divided, Rehoboam retaining the two tribes of Judah and Benjamin under his control and the remaining ten tribes of Israel which occupied the northern part of country became a separate kingdom under Jeroboam.[126]

Appendix 1 Alphabetical List of Characters

Abiathar	Priest. One of David's councillors
Abishag	Heroine of this story
Abishai	Heroic warrior in David's army
Abner	Saul's cousin. Commander of his army.
Absalom	David's rebellious son
Acsah	Mother of Abishag
Adonijah	David's fourth son
Ahimaaz	Son of Zadok
Ahithophel	David's treacherous counsellor and member of his council
Amasa	David's nephew. Briefly, commander of his army
Amnon	David's eldest son
Baanah	Murderer of Ishbosheph
Bathsheba	Wife of (1) Uriah (2) David
Benaiah	Hero of this story
David	King of Israel and Judah
Elhanan	Heroic warrior in David's army. Father of Abishag and Zalmon
Hushai	David's wise counsellor and member of his council
Hushim	Wife of Malcam who concealed Ahimaaz and Jonathan
Ishbosheph	Son of Saul
Jeroboam	Leader of revolt, later King of Israel

Jehoiada	(1) Father of Benaiah
	(2) Son of Benaiah and Abishag
Jerusha	Mother of Benaiah
Joab	David's nephew. Commander of his army
Jonadab	David's nephew
Jonathan	(1) Son of Saul (2) Son of Abiathar
Kileab	Second son of David who died young
Malcam	Supporter of David & husband of Hushim
Mephibosheph	(1) Son of Saul and Rizpah
	(2) Son of Jonathan
Michal	Daughter of Saul and wife of David
Paltiel	Husband of Michal
Recab	Brother of Baanah & fellow murderer of Ishbosheph
Rehoboam	King of Judah
Rizpah	Wife of (1) Saul (2) Abner
Samuel	Prophet who anointed (1) Saul (2) David
Saul	King of Israel and Judah
Solomon	Son of David. King of Israel and Judah
Tamar	Absalom's sister
Uriah	Husband of Bathsheba
Zadok	Priest. One of David's councillors
Zalmon	Renowned warrior, brother of Abishag and friend of Benaiah

Appendix 2 Genealogies & Family Trees

Family Tree of Benaiah and Abishag

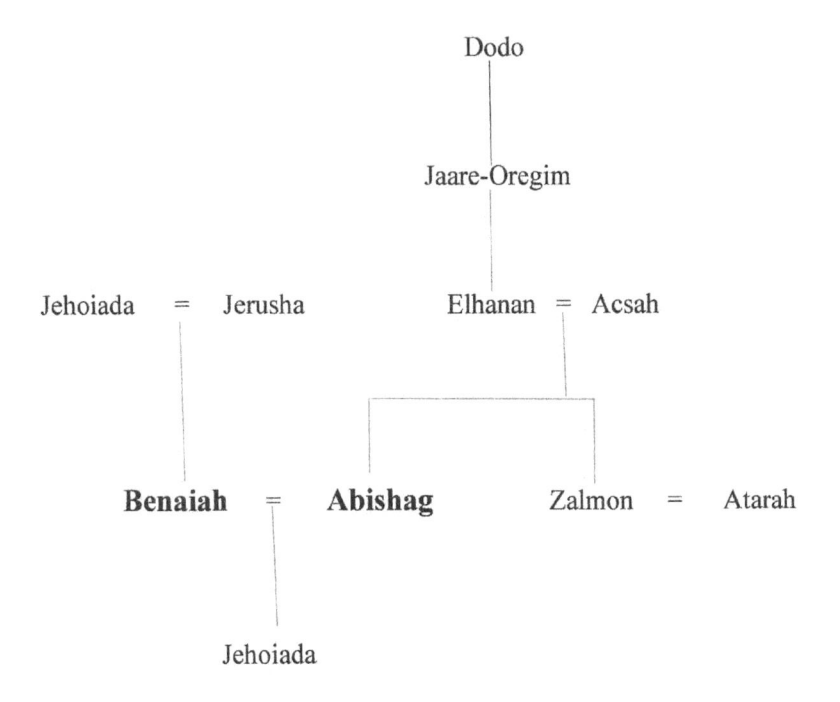

```
                              Dodo
                                |
                          Jaare-Oregim
                                |
Jehoiada  =  Jerusha      Elhanan  =  Acsah
       |                        |
       |          ┌─────────────┴──────┐
       |          |                    |
    Benaiah  =  Abishag          Zalmon  =  Atarah
            |
         Jehoiada
```

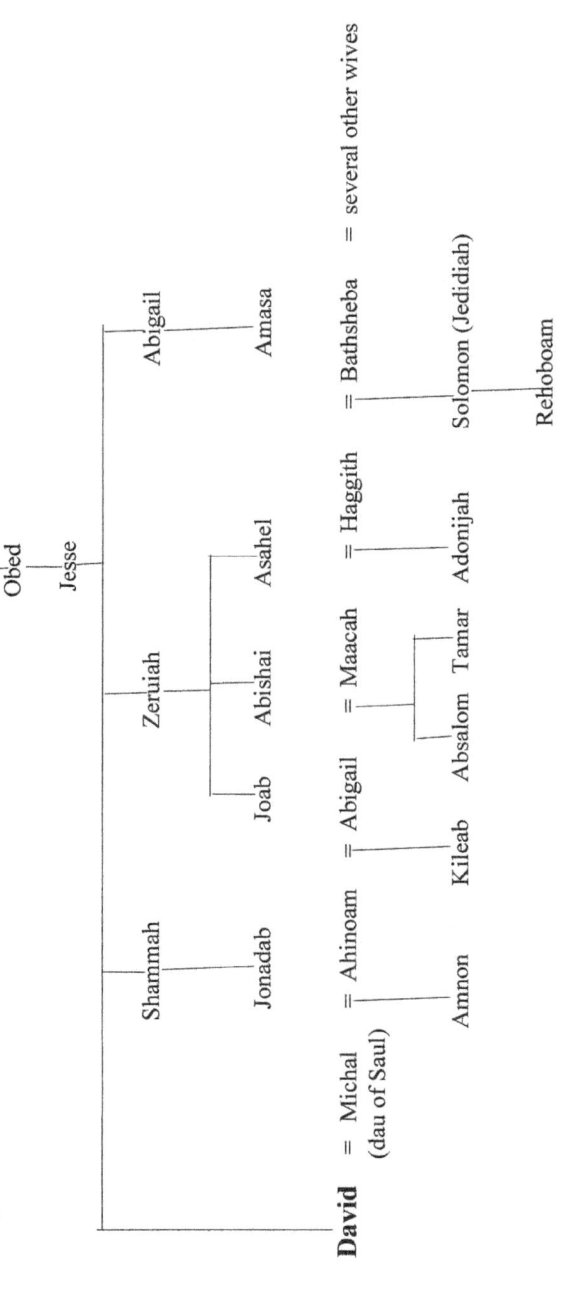

Family Tree of David

Salmon = Rahab
 └─ Boaz = Ruth
     └─ Obed
         └─ Jesse

Jesse's children: Shammah, Zeruiah, Abigail

Shammah
 └─ Jonadab

Zeruiah
 ├─ Joab
 ├─ Abishai
 └─ Asahel

Abigail
 └─ Amasa

David's wives and children:

- = Michal (dau of Saul)
- = Ahinoam → Amnon
- = Abigail → Kileab
- = Maacah → Absalom, Tamar
- = Haggith → Adonijah
- = Bathsheba → Solomon (Jedidiah) → Rehoboam
- = several other wives

Family Tree of Saul

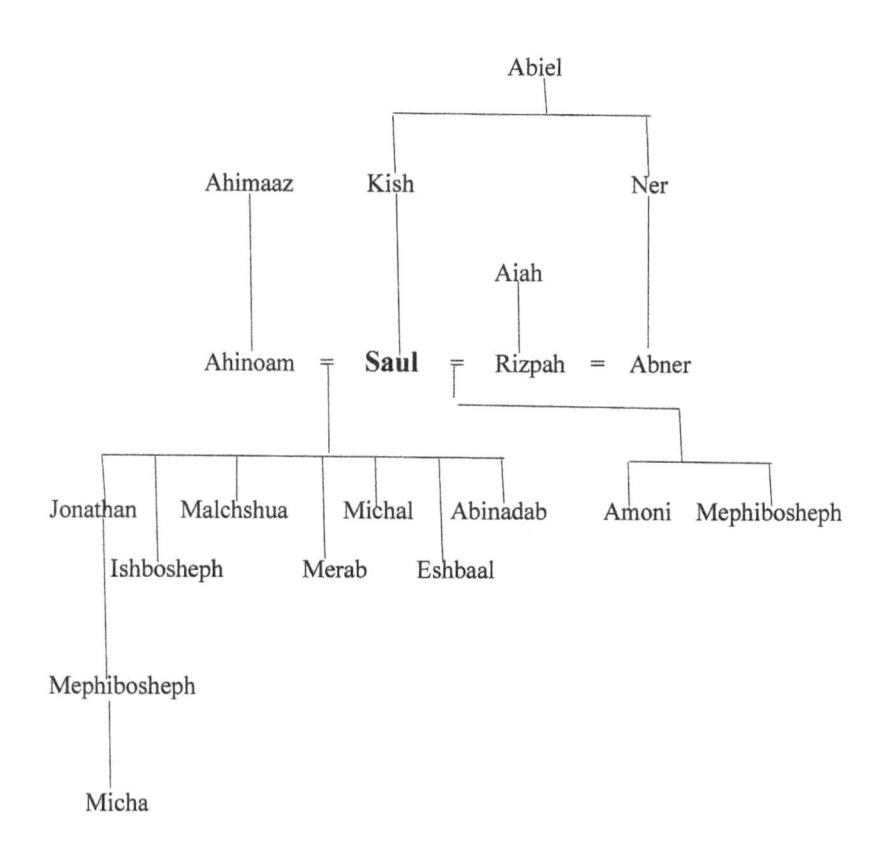

```
                        Abiel
                          |
         ┌────────────────┼────────────────┐
      Ahimaaz            Kish              Ner
                                  Aiah
                                   |
       Ahinoam  =  Saul  =  Rizpah  =  Abner
                   |                      |
   ┌──────┬────────┼────────┬──────┐   ┌──┴────────────┐
Jonathan Malchshua Michal Abinadab  Amoni  Mephibosheph
   |        Ishbosheph  Merab  Eshbaal
   |
Mephibosheph
   |
  Micha
```

Descent of Nations competing to occupy Israel

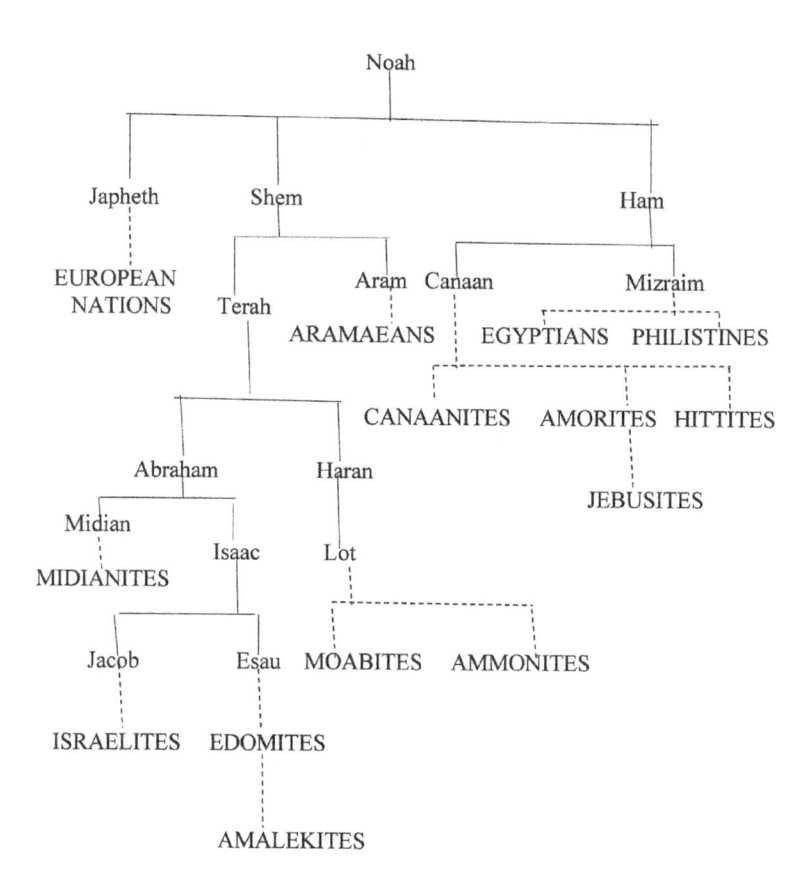

```
                              Noah
         ┌──────────────────────┼──────────────────────┐
      Japheth                 Shem                    Ham
         ┆              ┌──────┼──────┐          ┌─────┴─────┐
    EUROPEAN         Terah    Aram  Canaan              Mizraim
    NATIONS                    ┆                  ┌───────┼───────┐
                           ARAMAEANS           EGYPTIANS   PHILISTINES
                                         ┌──────────┼──────────┐
                                     CANAANITES  AMORITES   HITTITES
                                                    ┆
              ┌──────────┬──────────┐            JEBUSITES
          Abraham              Haran
         ┌──┴──┐                 │
      Midian  Isaac             Lot
         ┆    ┌──┴──┐         ┌──┴──┐
    MIDIANITES  │    │      MOABITES AMMONITES
              Jacob Esau
               ┆     ┆
          ISRAELITES EDOMITES
                     ┆
                 AMALEKITES
```

197

Appendix 3   Map showing approximate locations of places mentioned in the story

Appendix 4   Biblical References

1. 1 Samuel ch 31 v 1-7
2. Deuteronomy ch 34 v 1-4
3. 1 Samuel ch 18 v 13
4. 1 Samuel ch 30 v 6
5. 1 Samuel ch 30 v 7,8
6. 1 Samuel ch 30 v 9
7. 1 Samuel ch 30 v 11-15
8. 1 Samuel ch 30 v 18-20
9. 1 Samuel ch 30 v 21-24
10. 1 Samuel ch 29 v 2
11. 1 Samuel ch 29 v 27-31
12. 2 Samuel ch 1 v 1-16
13. 2 Samuel ch 3 v 1-5
14. 2 Samuel ch 2 v 3-17
15. 2 Samuel ch 2 v 18-23
16. 2 Samuel ch 2 v 25-27
17. 2 Samuel ch 3 v6-16
18. 2 Samuel ch 3 v 22-27
19. 2 Samuel ch 4 v 1-12
20. I Chronicles ch 11 v 17-19
21. I Chronicles ch 11 v 4-6
22. I Chronicles ch 14 v 1
23. I Chronicles ch 14 v 3-7
24. 2 Samuel ch 8 v 15-18

25. 2 Samuel ch 5 v 17-25
26. 1 Samuel ch 4 v 1-18
27. 1 Samuel ch 5 v 1-12
28. 1 Samuel ch 7 v 1
29. 2 Samuel ch 6 v 1-5
30. 2 Samuel ch 6 v 6-11
31. 2 Samuel ch 6 v 12-15
32. Exodus ch 25 v 8 – ch 26 v 31
33. 2 Samuel ch 6 v 20-23
34. 2 Samuel ch 7 v 1-2
35. 2 Samuel ch 7 v 4-17
36. 1 Chronicles ch 11 v 22
37. 2 Samuel ch 8 v 2
38. I Chronicles ch 11 v 23
39. 1 Chronicles ch 11 v 22
40. 2 Samuel ch 11 v 1
41. 2 Samuel ch 11 v 6-9
42. 2 Samuel ch 11 v 11-14
43. Judges ch 9 v 50-54
44. 2 Samuel ch 11 v 18-25
45. 2 Samuel ch 11 v 26-27
46. 2 Samuel ch 12 v 1-20
47. 2 Samuel ch 12 v 24-25
48. 2 Samuel ch 12 v 26-31
49. 1 Samuel ch 25 v 18-31

50. 2 Samuel ch 13 v 1-19
51. 2 Samuel ch 13 v 23-39
52. Joshua ch 4 v 1-9
53, Genesis ch 48 v 17-20
54. Genesis ch 34 v 25
55. Genesis ch 49 v 5-7
56. Genesis ch 23 v 7-20
57. Genesis ch 25 v 9,10
58. Genesis ch 49 v 29-32
59. Genesis ch 50 v 12-14
60. Genesis ch 11 v 4
61. Exodus ch 17 v 8-13
62 I Samuel ch 30 v 1
63. 2 Samuel ch 15 v 18
64. 2 Samuel ch 15 v 19-20
65. Genesis ch 22 v 18
66. Joshua ch 6 v 26
67. I Kings ch 16 v 34
68. Genesis ch 46 v 19
69. Matthew ch 1 v 5
70. Genesis ch 41 v 50
71. Exodus ch 2 v 21
72. 2 Samuel ch 14 v 1-20
73. 2 Samuel ch 14 v 21-23
74. 2 Samuel ch 14 v 28-29

75. 2 Samuel ch 14 v30-33
76. 2 Samuel ch 15 v 1-8
77. 2 Samuel ch 15 v 7-12
78. 2 Samuel ch 15 v 13-23
79. 2 Samuel ch 15 v 27-30
80. 2 Samuel ch 15 v 32-37
81. 2 Samuel ch 16 v 5-14
82. 2 Samuel ch 16 v 21
83. 2 Samuel ch 12 v 11
84. 2 Samuel ch 16 v 16-19
85. 2 Samuel ch 17 v 1-3
86. 2 Samuel ch 17 v 3-13
87. 2 Samuel ch 17 v 23
88. 2 Samuel ch 17 v 15-16
89. 2 Samuel ch 17 v 17-21
90. 2 Samuel ch 18 v 1-5
91. 2 Samuel ch 18 v 9-5
92. 2 Samuel ch 18 v 19-32
93. 2 Samuel ch 19 v 1-8
94. 2 Samuel ch 19 v 18-23
95. 2 Samuel ch 19 v 13
96. 2 Samuel ch 20 v 7
97. 2 Samuel ch 20 v 9-10
98. 2 Samuel ch 19 v 14-22
99. 2 Samuel ch 21 v 16

100. 2 Samuel ch 21 v 17
101. 2 Samuel ch 21 v 18-22
102. 1 Kings ch 1 v 1-4
103. 1 Kings ch 1 v 11-17
104. 1 Kings ch 1 v 17-27
105. 1 Kings ch 1 v 29-31
106. 1 Kings ch 1 v 32-35
107. 1 Kings ch 1 v 35-40
108. 1 Kings ch 1 v 41-50
109. 1 Kings ch 2 v 12-27
110. 1 Kings ch 2 v 26-27
111. 1 Kings ch 3 v 34
112. 1 Kings ch 2 v 28-34
113. 1 Kings ch 2 v 35
114. 1 Kings ch 2 v 35-46
115. 2 Samuel ch 20 v 3
116. 2 Samuel ch 23 v 28
117. John ch 14 v 4
118. Judges ch 4 v 14-16
119. 1 Kings ch 4 v 26
120 1 Kings ch 6 v1-38
121. 1 Kings ch 6 v 1-12
122. 1 Kings ch 11 v 1-8
123. 1 Kings ch 11 v 28
124. 1 Kings ch 11 v 29-39

125. 1 Kings ch 11 v 40
126. 1 Kings ch 12 v 1-17
127. Genesis ch 29 v 25
128. Matthew ch 26 v 29
129. Matthew ch 25 v 1-12

Appendix 5

Bibliography

Holy Bible – New International Version
　　　　　　　　Hodder & Stoughton 1979

He Illustrated Bible Dictionary, Parts 1,2 & 3
　　　　　　　　Inter-Varsity Press 1994

Strong's Concordance of the Bible
　　　　　　　　Thomas Nelson 1985

The Ancient Jewish Wedding by Jamie Lash
　　　　　　　　Jewish Jewels 2012

The books published by Midhurst have been written by Dr Ray Filby who has had many years' experience of church life in a number of churches, fulfilling at various times the roles of Pathfinder Group Leader, Youth Fellowship Leader, Secretary to the Parochial Church Council, Churchwarden and Reader (Licensed Lay Minister). This experience is reflected in the stories he writes which embrace several genres, including historical fiction, short stories, Bible study, murder stories and romantic fiction. They are all available from Amazon in paperback or Kindle form.

The Sun and the Moon of Alexandria

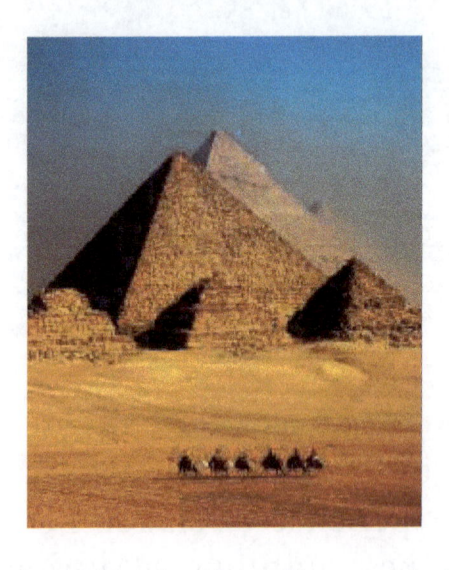

This is a fictional biopic of Apollos, a missionary saint and one of St. Paul's co-workers. Although mentioned many times in the New Testament, little is known of the life and background of Apollos. Thus, there is scope to create a story which constructs a feasible account of Apollos' youth in Egypt, his journey to Israel, his conversion, his relationship with St. Paul, his missionary work and his marriage. The story culminates in his martyrdom. In situations where Apollos interacts with well-known Biblical characters, the narrative remains faithful to the New Testament account.

(This book is published by the Book Guild)

Parables, the Greatest Stories ever told - Retold

'The Greatest Stories ever told – Retold' focuses on the better known parables of Jesus and rewrites them as situations in modern life which correspond to the situations in Jesus' day, attempting to promote the same teaching that Jesus was giving in the original parable. Each parable is preceded by a modern translation of the original parable and followed by ten questions which are suitable for a person's private devotions or for use in the context of a group Bible study.

St. Columba's – Its Life and Its People

Churches are living organisms, each with their own distinctive patterns of life. While their members experience the same ups and downs in life as the population as a whole, their Christian faith results in their reacting to circumstances in a distinctive way.

This book is a set of short stories, some of which trace the unfolding of events which occur as part of church life, and others which recount the experience of individual church members. Readers are invited to consider the practical or ethical problems which arise in these stories and think how they themselves might have dealt with or reacted to these situations.

The Countess who should have been Queen

Margaret Plantagenet was born near the end of the Wars of the Roses. As the daughter of the brother of King Edward IV, a situation could well have arisen when she or her brother, Edward, had a claim to the throne. Margaret was not ambitious to become Queen but was happy to marry a commoner and settled as an enlightened landowner with her husband in Berkshire. Margaret became Queen Catherine of Aragon's chief lady-in-waiting and was awarded a peerage to become Countess of Salisbury. Margaret faithfully supported Catherine right through her reign and as far as she could when Catherine was sent to live in isolation after her divorce. One of Margaret's sons, Reginald, became a prominent churchman and angered the King by writing a treatise, heavily critical of Henry VIII, the way he had divorced Catherine and taken over the Church of England. Reginald was living out of reach of Henry on the continent so Henry vented his wrath on Margaret and her family.

Consequences of Immature Love

Boy-Girl, Man-Woman relationships cement our society. Because these relationships are seldom straightforward, they provide scope for an indefinite number of works of fiction. In this novel, you are invited to follow the amorous adventures of Georgina Matthews and Arthur Gray from the time they leave school and start at university until they ultimately marry the partner for whom they seemed destined from the outset.

The story told might be of special interest to a young person embarking on the minefield of love and courtship as they consider the factors which led to the success or failure of the relationships encountered in this novel. Ethical factors are involved and it is significant that a shared Christian faith led to the final happy outcome.

Soldiers, Saints and Sinners

'Soldiers, Saints and Sinners' is a collection of fictitious stories, featuring some of the minor characters whom Jesus encountered in his ministry. It attempts to suggest how their backgrounds might have been important in the way they led to their encounter with Jesus and the way these encounters furthered the progress of Jesus' ministry. Each story is preceded by a modern Biblical translation of the passage which recounts their appearance on the scene where Jesus was ministering and is followed by five questions which are suitable for a person's private devotions or for use in the context of a group Bible study.

The Tasks of Chronavon

When sensible twelve-year-olds, Alfred and Alice meet a mysterious angel called Chronavon in the vestry of their church, it seems someone is playing a practical joke on them. After all, angels don't just pop up in church vestries to enlist the help of two young people to journey back in time to prevent a devilish time traveller from altering the course of history. Yet it soon becomes clear that Chronavon's incredible story is true. As Alfred and Alice are whisked backwards through the centuries, they become immersed in the rich customs and costumes of the past through Henry III's troubled reign, the insecurity of Princess Elizabeth before she became Queen Elizabeth I and the Civil War between the Cavaliers and Roundheads. 'The Tasks of Chronavon' is an exciting, informative tale for young readers which effortlessly weaves fact and fiction with a sprinkling of humour and shows how little human values have changed over time.

The Evil Occupants of Easingdale Castle

Teenager, Jason, and his friends, Bill, Becky and Liz, are recruited by an unusual messenger to pit their wits against an international gang of forgers, occupying their local castle. The gang are intent on destabilising the British economy by flooding the country with forged £20 notes which could pass off as the real thing. The gang is well equipped with hi-tech machines.

It remains to be seen whether Jason and his friends, who are also technically knowledgeable, can outwit the gang.

Technology will have advanced since this book was written and young readers are invited to consider whether they could have done better than Jason and his friends with equipment now available.

The Evil Emir of Transoxiana

Becky meets with her special friends, Jason, Bill and Liz, to tell them she is being posted to Transoxiana. She needs to explain exactly where she will be working, that she will be accompanied by Jason and that she will be spending some time with her Kyrgyz penfriend, Askari, and her husband, Temier.

During Becky's stay with Askari, Temier falls foul of an extremist Islamic cleric, the self-styled, Emir of Transoxiana. The resourcefulness of Becky and Jason, helped by Bill and Liz who travel out to join them, is needed to keep Askari and Temier safe from the Evil Emir. In spite of the danger being faced, they all manage to have the experiences in Transoxiana which make their stay both exciting and enjoyable.

A Church like Cluedo

After graduating from college as a civil engineer, Annette Owen had hoped to work in the developing world under the auspices of a missionary society. When this door to Christian service was closed, she applied to become an ordained minister but was turned down by the selection committee. She was however able to exercise a very fulfilled ministry as a clergy wife. Unfortunately, her clergy husband had dark secrets in his life of which Annette was totally unaware until a situation arose which resulted in murder being committed. The impact of this had an unexpected effect on the course of Annette's life.

Inspector Sinclair and Sergeant Powers' most interesting cases

This account of some interesting cases solved by the detective duo, Inspector Sinclair and Sergeant Powers, is not a normal 'whodunnit' in which the murderer is not revealed until the very end when the detective reveals the clues which he or she alone has picked up to solve the case without sharing their significance with the reader until the very end.

The stories in this book are divided into sections, a list of those involved to help the reader keep track of the characters,

'the Event' which describes the situation when the murder took place,

'the Investigation' which describes the systematic way in which the detectives investigated the case and

'the Evidence' in which the crucial evidence by which a cast iron case against the murderer was built up, is reviewed.

An Insight into the Gospels and the Book of Acts

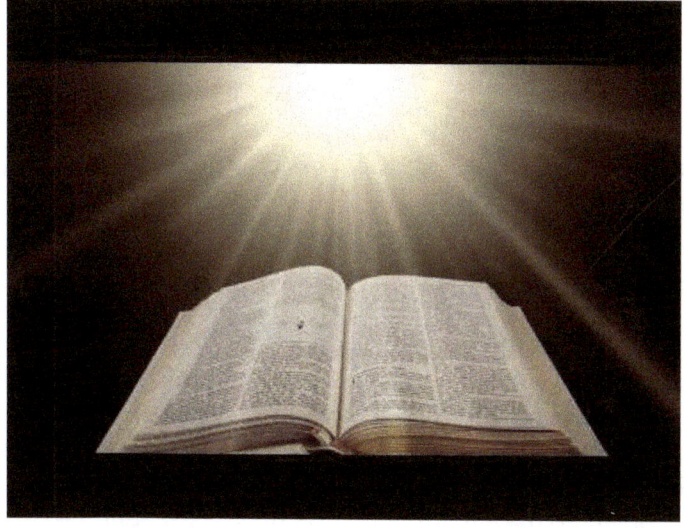

'An Insight into the Gospels and the Book of Acts' is an overview of the themes, contents, emphases, and structure of the first five books of the New Testament. While there is so much similarity in the stories and teaching in each of the gospels, this book contrasts the way each gospel is written and presented. It highlights the quite remarkable differences which exist between each of the gospels as they are directed to different audiences and have different primary objectives. The book is presented with the main content of the book appearing on the right hand (odd numbered) pages and supportive texts placed opposite the relevant passages on the left hand pages.

Puzzles, Quiz and Activities Suitable for Social Events
Volumes 1, 2, 3 & 4

These books consist of a set of puzzles, quiz and activities which the author designed for use at a monthly social event organised by St. Michael's, Church, Budbrooke, in the Community Centre in the part of the parish known as Chase Meadow. People who have opted to take part really seem to have enjoyed these activities which are interesting rather than extremely challenging. While a good general knowledge is helpful in completing some of the activities, they are not designed to expose people's ignorance as data sheets and appropriate reference books like atlases are made available to help participants find any information needed. Thus, the activities are educational.

The socials run at Chase Meadow are not restricted to church members but all and sundry are invited as part of the church outreach. With many of the activities, a final stage often involves deciphering a phrase, quote or saying. As the socials are sponsored by the church, many of the quotes to be deciphered are Biblical texts. However, anyone choosing to use these ideas could quite easily modify the final stage and use a secular quote rather than a Biblical text to be deciphered.

Lightning Source UK Ltd.
Milton Keynes UK
UKHW022344090822
407084UK00006B/121